SOMEONE ELSE'S LIFE

WHAT IF YOU WEREN'T WHO YOU THOUGHT YOU WERE?

KEVIN J SIMINGTON

KEVIN J SIMINGTON

CONTENTS

KEVIN J SIMINGTON

EDITORS: Tony Baker, Sandra Simington

❋ Created with Vellum

1

———————

It's surprising how uncomfortable it is, sitting on top of someone. I've been straddling this guy for four and a half minutes now, and my back is starting to ache. That's because I'm leaning slightly forward with my right thumb buried in his posterior cutaneous nerve at the base of his right trapezius muscle. My left hand also has a firm grip on his left thumb which is currently bent at a painful angle and is half-way up the guy's back, close to his shoulder blade. He hasn't tried to move for at least two minutes now, which is comforting, but I wish he would stop cursing. Gratuitous gutter language isn't my thing. The English language is replete with such a vast array of diverse and expressive adjectives that I find it puzzling why people resort to the same few guttural expletives to describe just about everything.

The guy lets loose with another obscenity, which he apparently believes will convince me of the injustice of my current treatment of him.

"No," I respond calmly, "I don't have sex with my mother. You must be confusing me with your brother."

That seems to have gotten under his skin. He arches his

back and tries to dislodge me, letting fly with a few more meaningless references to sexual intercourse in general and the female genitals in particular, but I simply dig a little deeper into his nerve and he screams in agony. He submits again, begging for me to ease off, which I do. His face is back on the pavement now, turned slightly to the side, with blood and snot running from his nose and pooling against his cheek.

There are two onlookers now. The latest arrival, an overweight man in dirty tracksuit pants and wearing sandals and socks, is looking into the open door of the shop and seems about to enter.

"Don't go in there! He's dead! It's a crime scene. Stay out here."

As I say it, I hear the sirens at last. It took them long enough. The other onlooker, a teenage girl who witnessed the murder along with me, phoned the cops as soon as it happened and has been standing on the sidewalk chewing gum and recording us ever since. I think I'm going to be featured in her next upload to Tweetify or Instapost or whatever is the latest 'Look At My Life, Isn't It Amazing!' social media platform. She'll probably write something like 'OMG! WTF! Check this shit out!'

The cops arrive at last; three cars in quick succession. Our fearless law enforcers emerge with guns drawn and immediately save the day by screaming at me to get my hands in the air. There must be some course in basic training that has been scrapped due to budget cuts: *How to Recognize the Bad Guys.*' I continue to hold down the bad guy, because he'll be up and running like a rabbit if I let him go. The cops have all taken cover behind their cars, at least ten yards away, their guns all levelled at my back. Apparently, my butt is a lethal weapon that could blow them all to kingdom come.

"Put your hands in the air now, or we will shoot!"

The Training Academy has apparently also axed the '*How to Avoid Shooting Innocent People*' course.

"I'll be very happy to raise my arms in the air, if one of you brave officers could come and cuff this guy."

Twenty minutes later, I've managed to avoid getting shot, and the scene is awash with red and blue flashing lights. I'd really like to go home now, but I know how all this works. I'll be lucky to be in bed by dawn. I've already given my statement to an officer who laboriously transcribed my description of events using a pen and notepad. Maybe the police department hasn't heard of smart phones and recording apps.

Although it's nearly midnight, a crowd of about thirty people has gathered on the sidewalk, held back by police tape. Many of them are holding their smartphones out in front, like worshippers at a temple, offering their own cinematic contributions to the gods of social media. Fortunately, the body is out of sight on the floor behind the counter, but the shelves of cigarettes on the wall behind are covered in blood and brain matter. Judging by the width of the splatter pattern, the pistol was probably loaded with 147 grain hollow points.

A forensic team has taken charge of the 7-Eleven store, photographing, measuring and dusting for fingerprints – although I have no idea why they're bothering with fingerprints, as the perpetrator is already safely in custody. A medical examiner and her assistant are standing outside the door, waiting for the forensic team to finish. I'm not sure why they need to be here: it's not as though the cause of death is in any doubt. Two ambulance officers are also waiting their turn, sitting on the rear bumper of their vehicle smoking cigarettes; a wonderful visual contradiction.

Just as I'm starting to think that I might be able to sneak home, an unmarked police car with blue strobing lights pulls up and two plain clothes officers get out. They speak with one of the uniformed officers for several minutes and he then points them toward me. They walk over to me.

Here we go. Round two.

"Mr. Targett, I'm Detective Abrams and this is Detective Rosario. We'd like to ask you a few questions if you don't mind."

"Can I see your identification, please?"

I like to ask for official ID, not because I don't believe them but simply because it's my right as a citizen.

"What? The unmarked police car not good enough for you?" sneers Rosario.

I just smile and stand my ground.

They pull out their IDs and shove them toward me. Detective Eva Rosario and Senior Detective Elijah Abrams. I nod and thank them.

"Mr. Targett, can you describe again what took place?" asks Abrams.

There's no point in mentioning that I've already given a full statement to the patrol officer, so I go over the facts again. Abrams then starts asking questions.

"Apparently you weren't in the shop at the time of the murder. Do you mind telling us what you were doing in the vicinity at this time of night?"

"I'm working a case for a client."

"You're a P.I.?"

"Yes."

I notice Rosario roll her eyes. Police officers don't tend to like private investigators. It's as if we are an insult to their own vocation, taking up the slack because they can't do their job properly.

"Who is your client?"

"I don't have to answer that question."

I am also aware that the answer would only increase Rosario's scorn because it would highlight the often-petty nature of my cases. I was working for the shop owner who was convinced that one of his employees was smoking cigarettes inside the store while he was on the late-night shift. I had suggested installing cameras inside the shop but the owner, a Pakistani man, was convinced that the government would be able to hack into them. So I had been sitting in my car in the parking lot, freezing my cojones off, fifty yards from the shop, when the attempted robbery had taken place.

Abrams seems to accept my refusal to answer, but I can sense Rosario's hackles rising. At about 5'8", she has short-cropped, dark hair, olive complexion and a lean face with harsh features. Dressed all in black, she seems to be going for the Cat-Woman look, and I feel like telling her that she's not pulling it off very well at all. Abrams is a couple of inches shorter, a few decades older and at least forty pounds heavier. His gray trousers and gray cardigan are speckled with food stains and his gaudily striped shirt looks like it was a reject from a church thrift shop. Abrams lets his question about my case pass and moves on.

"What's with the accent?" asks Rosario. "Are you British?"

"Born in Australia. Lived there until I was ten. Then we lived in London until I was fifteen."

"So, you're a visitor in our country," she says aggressively.

"I'm an American citizen. Dual citizenship. My father was American."

Rosario grunts dismissively and shakes her head, as if this doesn't count. Abrams ignores Rosario's hostility and continues trying to piece together what happened.

"So you were conducting surveillance from your car?"

"Yes," I say, pointing to the decrepit Subaru Forester which looks in similar shape to Abrams himself.

Abrams looks back and forth between the car and the sidewalk where I had apprehended the perpetrator, gauging the distance.

"You must have reacted pretty quickly."

I nod. "Uh huh." What can I say? I'm fast when I need to be.

"Then you disarmed the suspect and made a citizen's arrest."

"That's correct."

Rosario speaks up at this point.

"Seems to me you were a little too enthusiastic in your citizen's arrest, Mr. Targett. He's got a badly broken nose. You could be up on assault charges."

So there it is. She can't help herself. An intrinsic need to assert her dominance through threat and intimidation. She's the classic profile of the ego-driven detective. I smile at her in what I hope she recognizes as a condescending manner.

"You might also want to check for fractures of the right ulnar, the right thumb metacarpal, and I'm pretty sure I broke at least one of his ribs, number seven or eight on the left."

Rosario blinks, momentarily nonplussed.

I smile again. "You're welcome, by the way."

"Like I said," persists Rosario, "possible assault charges."

"Well, detective, I did consider engaging in a philosophical discussion with the perpetrator regarding the dangers of firearms and the decidedly antisocial nature of blowing someone's brains out, but as he was bringing his pistol to bear on me I took a wild guess and deduced that he wasn't in the mood for a chat."

Abrams glances at Rosario and gives her a look that seems to suggest that she back off. He turns to me and speaks in a more placatory manner.

"You obviously have some training in self-defense."

"I get by."

He nods. He checks his notebook for a moment and then snaps it closed.

"I think that's all the information we need for now, Mr. Targett. We've got your address and personal details, as well as your statement to the patrol officer. We'll be examining the

CCTV footage from outside the store and we'll be in contact if we have any further questions. We'll need you to come down to the station tomorrow sometime and sign a statement, if you don't mind."

I watch as they walk away, Rosario striding purposefully and Abrams walking with a slight limp, favoring his right leg. I walk back to my car, hoping like hell the cantankerous old beast will start.

2

———

It's Saturday morning and I've got a class starting at 9:00 am. I get up, feeling like I've hardly slept, and dive under the shower. The hot water system has packed it in again, and the cold water hits me like an electric shock. I have the shortest shower in history, blowing and snorting like a horse that has just done a two-mile gallop. There's no time to shave, but as I dry myself, I glance in the mirror and note that my two-day stubble is now approaching what many would consider to be a fashionable length. I've never understood the fashion myself. It probably started when some hung-over pop star couldn't be bothered shaving and everyone else decided that they wanted to be a unique individual just like him. My hair needs a cut too, although if Jessie were here, she would tell me that my collar-length scruffy dark hair and blue eyes were what initially attracted her to me. I always thought it was my superior intellect and wit. I notice a few more gray hairs at my temple and shake my head. At thirty nine years of age, it's all downhill from here.

I throw last night's clothes on, grab my keys and head downstairs. We live in a two-bedroom apartment above two shops; one of the shops is my office and the other is a coffee shop. I lock the door to the apartment at the top of the stairs and head down. The cracked and dirty tiled stairs descend steeply to a tiny foyer below. To the right is a glass door into my office and straight ahead is the glass door that opens onto the sidewalk. I unlock the latter and turn right. Walking past the darkened front window of my office, I come to the coffee shop located on the street corner and directly underneath my lounge room. The Beanstalk isn't exactly the hippest coffee shop in town, but what it lacks in urban 'hipness' it makes up for with the quality of its coffee and the warmth of the owner. Costa is like a caricature of the classic Greek fruit shop owner, except he only sells one fruit – the dried, roasted berry of the coffee bush. He is a barrel-chested man with an infectious, effervescent nature and a booming voice.

I check my watch. I've just got time for a coffee. There are two people standing in line, and the young barista and even younger-looking sales assistant are hard at work. I pause in the doorway, thinking that I won't have time to wait in line, but Costa sees me and waves me in, already moving toward the coffee machine as he does so.

"Ah, Mr. John! Good morning! Come in, come in!" For some reason he has never referred to me by my surname, and never by my first name alone.

"What would you like today?"

"Double decaf caramel latte, thanks Costa." It's a game we play; a daily ritual that hasn't changed for five years.

"No problem, Mr. John. Coming right up!" He shoves his barista out of the way and takes over, expertly working the machine and handing me a strong black coffee with no sugar.

"How is it?" he asks, as I take a sip. This, too, is part of our ritual.

"The best you've ever made, Costa."

"Ah! Good! I thought so. I'll put it on your tab."

Of course, there is no tab and there never will be. I've never been able to pay for a coffee at the Beanstalk and I've given up trying. I had several conversations with Costa in the early days, assuring him that just because I was his landlord, I didn't expect free coffee, but he would not be deterred. All his staff are under strict instructions to never accept any money from me. I even tried going to another coffee shop to avoid taking advantage of Costa's generosity, but after several days of my buying coffee from the opposition, Costa somehow found out and came to see me, asking why I didn't like his coffee anymore and whether he had done something to offend me. In the end, I surrendered to his generosity. He is a good man and in the five years that I've owned the building, we've developed an easy friendship.

I walk around the corner to the parking lot at the rear of the building. The parking lot opens off a laneway that runs behind all the shops and offices for the entire block. Costa's car and another one are parked behind the coffee shop near the rear entrance, and my beat up Subaru is waiting doggedly by the back door to my office. Surprisingly, it starts first time, and ten minutes later I'm setting up the dummies and mats in the nearby YMCA hall.

It's the second week of the three-week course. Over the years I've learnt that three weeks is enough to cover the basics and give them the skills and awareness that might one day save their lives. I vary the courses between nights and weekends. I run one course for the first three Saturday mornings of one month, and the next course for the first three Tuesday nights on the following month, with a week off for me in the middle. I donate my time freely and the women aren't charged for the course. People probably think I'm generous or community-minded or motivated by some other virtuous quality, but they're wrong. I don't do this out of the goodness of my heart. I'm driven by guilt.

As 9:00 am approaches, all six women arrive at virtually the same time and we get underway with a quick review of the first lesson, which was 'responding to a frontal assault'. It must have made a big impression, because they can all list off the five most effective responses to an attack from the front: head butt, palm strike to the nose, and the three all-time favorites – the nut-cracker, nut-smasher and nut-masher.

"Who can tell me the difference between the three nut strikes?" I ask, and the women all chuckle. Janine, the freckled red head, calls out enthusiastically,

"The nut-cracker is a knee to the balls, the nut-smasher is a kick using the point of your shoe and a nut-masher is a hand grab and squeeze."

As she says this, she holds a hand out in front and squeezes her fingers together with a look of intense satisfaction on her face. The other women all laugh.

"Excellent! My testicles have just shriveled to the size of raisins, watching that!"

The women break up into hilarious laughter.

"Remember," I say, "striking a man's groin is the most effective means of disabling him so that you can make a getaway, and the proximity of the attacker to you will determine which of those three nut strikes you use."

I divide them into pairs and get them to do a quick refresher of those moves, with one woman holding the life-sized dummy while the other attacks it, then swapping over. It is always surreal watching ordinary women – housewives, mothers, daughters and sometimes even grandmothers – transformed into aggressive defenders. But this is the number one lesson I drilled into them last week: the need to be instantly aggressive, to strike hard and fast. Waiting for the situation to escalate before acting could cost a woman her life.

The main part of this week's lesson is responding to being grabbed or held from behind. Using a dummy held up by one of the women, I demonstrate the reverse headbutt, the upward head butt (into the jaw of a taller attacker) the side elbow strike to the temple and the heel rake – scraping your shoe down the shin of the attacker and stamping on their foot. The women then break into twos again and practice for a while. Then I get them to combine the skills from the two weeks, using one of today's techniques to break the hold of a rear attacker and then spinning around to disable them with one of the offensive moves.

It's a good lesson, and the women work enthusiastically. With fifteen minutes to go, I see that a sergeant from the Police Liaison Unit has arrived for her ten-minute talk. Last week a doctor from the local hospital spoke to the women about rape. This week, Sergeant Debbi Gleeson will give a ten-minute talk about assault and femicide – the alarming rise of women being assaulted and murdered in the United States. I pack up the equipment as the sergeant outlines to the women the alarming statistics and provides some valuable pointers about how to avoid becoming victims themselves.

As the class breaks up, an attractive blonde comes up to me and thanks me for the lesson. I vaguely recall that her name is Asha. I studiously avoid all physical contact with participants in my classes and try to shut down any flirtatious overtures that come my way, but I've been picking up a certain vibe from her since the very beginning.

"You were very impressive last night," she says, touching my arm lightly.

I am momentarily confused. Did I miss something? I was nowhere near her last night. She senses my confusion.

"The YouTube video. You captured that murderer. You were amazing."

"It's on YouTube?"

"Yes. It's had over a million views already."

I shake my head, still processing. It must have been that girl with the smartphone.

"Plus, the clip was shown on the news this morning as well. They mentioned your name. You're famous."

How did they get my name? By the time I left the crime scene last night, there were several news teams with cameras and reporters setting up, but I managed to avoid them. They must have gotten my name from one of the cops.

I politely disentangle myself from Asha's clinging presence, telling her that I'll see her next week. As I walk through the foyer, Jimmy, the middle-aged guy who mans the front desk, calls over to me.

"Hey John. Are you sure you can't fit more than six women to a session? Your classes are booked up for the next six months and there's a waiting list as long as my arm."

He points to the sign-up sheet on the noticeboard, which is headed, 'Women's Self-Defense Classes: A 3-week course that could save your life.'

"It's limited by the number of dummies we've got, Jimmy." I respond. "If you can somehow get us some more, I'm happy to have bigger classes."

"OK. I'll see what I can do."

I get in my car and spend several minutes coaxing it to life, then drive home, looking forward to a quiet remainder of the morning.

It wasn't going to happen.

3

"What the hell?" I say out loud, as I drive past my office and turn the corner toward the rear parking lot. There's a small crowd staking out my office: reporters and camera operators. Clearly, they're not very intelligent, though, because no one is waiting for me around the back. I park the car and let myself into my office via the back door.

When I bought the dilapidated building five years ago, Costa had just opened the Beanstalk, and the shop I now use as my office had been untenanted for eighteen months. Its last use had been as a dress shop, specializing in Balinese tie-dye clothing. I have yet to see a single woman wearing Balinese tie-dye dresses in the Santa Clara area.

The back door opens into a disused storeroom at the rear, then into a short corridor. There are two doors on the right – a toilet and a small shower room – and a basic kitchen area on the left, featuring a sink, a bar fridge, a tired old combination oven and stove, and a rusty microwave oven that looks like it belongs in a museum. The short hallway ends with a shabby piece of cloth – green and orange stripes – that serves as a curtain, separating the hall from the open office area in front. I push through the curtain and enter my office. There are two desks. Don't ask me why. It's only me who works here. I picked them up from a second-hand furniture store and the guy sold me the second one for an extra twenty bucks. I'm a sucker for a bargain.

As I move through the office toward the glass door that opens into the foyer, I give silent thanks that I remembered to lock the door to the street, but this doesn't stop the reporters hammering on the glass door and calling out to me when they see me. I ignore them and all they get is a glimpse of my back as I walk up the stairs. I quickly unlock the door to my apartment at the top of the stairs and breathe a sigh of relief as I close the door behind me. My fifteen-year-old daughter is sitting at the breakfast bar eating a bowl of cereal.

"You're awake!" I say, failing to keep the note of incredulity out of my voice. I glance at the clock on the wall. It's 10:20. Addie doesn't usually surface until at least 11:00 on a Saturday.

"How could I not be?" she answers. "The whole world's been banging on the door downstairs for the last hour. Plus, you left your phone here again! Don't you ever take it with you, Dad? I had to switch it to silent. It's been ringing off its clacker!"

"I didn't know it had a clacker," I respond. "Can it be replaced if it wears out?"

"Ha, ha. You're hilarious."

"Thanks. I try my best."

"Seriously, Dad! You're freakin' famous! Have you seen the video?"

"No."

"Holy crap! It's all over the internet. You've gotta watch it! Check it out."

I walk across to the kitchen bench where she is currently sitting in her fleecy pajamas and slippers eating a bowl of Froot Loops. I take the stool next to her. Her thumbs fly across the surface of her smartphone and then the video starts.

It was obviously recorded by the gum-chewing teenage girl last night. She must have already been recording herself, standing outside the shop, because at first all we see is her face and then there is the sound of a gun blast from inside. The screen swings around wildly, while the girl can be heard swearing, over and over again. A few moments go by, with the girl's panicked voice now saying, "I'm gonna die! I'm gonna die!". The screen then stabilizes. She is apparently now hiding behind a trash can a few yards further along the sidewalk and she points her camera toward the entrance of the store just as the perpetrator emerges. He's dressed in scruffy jeans and a dark hoodie, and he emerges from the shop holding the pistol in his right hand and two cartons of cigarettes in his left. He seems momentarily confused, not sure which way to run. As he looks left then right, I come onto the scene.

I'm sprinting at full speed and I launch myself into the air with my right foot extended out in front, in a classic flying kick. That's when I broke the guy's ribs. He lands hard on his back but he still has the gun in his hand and I'm now standing over him. As he starts to swing the gun up toward me, I execute a roundhouse kick, smashing my right boot into his right wrist, which sends the gun flying and probably fractures his ulnar. The momentum of the kick has me pivoting to the left so I make a split-second decision to continue the rotation because I can see that the guy is now trying to get up. As I continue to pivot, I sit down heavily on his chest, with my back now toward him, and use the remaining lateral momentum to swing my left elbow around and down behind me in an elbow strike to his face. That's when I broke his nose.

It was all over in less than two seconds. The rest is a simple tidy-up operation, rolling the guy onto his stomach and restraining him with one arm behind his back. The whole time, chewing-gum girl can be heard saying "Oh my God!" interspersed with other equally original expressions, over and over again.

"Holy crap, Dad! That was freakin' awesome!"

"Do you want to rephrase that in a more articulate manner?"

"That was a particularly impressive feat, Father dearest."

"Much better," I say, kissing her on the forehead.

I look closely at the screen and see the description underneath it, obviously posted by the girl who filmed it. 'OMG! You'll never guess WJHTM! This is insane! WTF!'

"WJHTM?" I ask.

"What just happened to me."

"Ah. I see. What a wonderful world it is when we no longer have to speak whole words to each other. WEWYLFB."

"What?" Addie asks, looking confused.

"What else would you like for breakfast?"

"Ha, ha. Pancakes if you're making them. But no bacon, otherwise I'll spew my guts up at soccer later."

"Delightful," I say, moving into the kitchen and starting preparations.

It's been just Addison and me in the apartment for five years now, and I'm still learning what it means to be a solo parent. I love her to bits and she is my whole life, but I worry that I'm not doing a great job. A girl needs a mother. Addie is fifteen, going on twenty-one, and I am completely out of my depth with her. She is at that awkward stage of no longer being a little girl, but not yet being a woman, and I can sense her desperately trying to work out who she is. Sometimes she will still snuggle up beside me on a Friday or Saturday night, eating popcorn and watching a movie with me. But those times are becoming rarer. Increasingly she wants space and freedom and privacy, and I seem to have misplaced the guidebook on how to manage all of that as a parent.

I flick the TV on as I start to cook the pancakes, and I'm just in time to see my face heading up the next news bulletin.

"An extraordinary video has emerged this morning of the capture of an armed gunman who had just murdered a shop assistant at a 7-Eleven store in Santa Clara, California. The gunman was disarmed and captured by an unarmed citizen who just happened to be on the scene when the murder occurred. The hero of the moment is John Targett, a private investigator and martial arts instructor who can be seen here executing an extraordinary series of moves ..."

I turn the TV off.

"Don't you want to watch it?" Addie asks.

"No."

"Why not? I think it's amazing."

"You won't think it's so amazing when we try to leave here in a couple of hours to get you to soccer."

I wasn't wrong.

4

A couple of hours later, I'm walking down the stairs with Addie, trying to work out what scares me the most; having to shoulder our way through a crush of reporters to get to our car, or having to fend off the two single soccer moms who have me firmly in their sights. I think I prefer the reporters.

There's a bunch of them still waiting on the sidewalk outside the front door and they start yelling and flashing cameras at us as we descend the stairs. We get to the bottom of the stairs and turn right, into my office, and start making our way toward the back door. The reporters, however, aren't going to be caught out a second time. There must have been some already waiting in the back parking lot, because as we open the back door, we are greeted by at least four reporters with accompanying camera operators, and the ones from around the front soon join them. I manage to get Addie into the car while they are jostling us and yelling questions at me, and then I make a snap decision. These people are going to keep hounding us until I speak with them, so I decide to give them a few moments.

"Mr. Targett, can you tell us how you felt while you were apprehending the murderer? Weren't you afraid for your own life?"

"There wasn't time to be afraid."

"What made you do it?"

"It was the right thing to do. He'd just shot an innocent man."

"Mr. Targett, do you think you were unnecessarily violent in your apprehension of the suspect."

"Firstly, he wasn't merely a suspect: I'd just seen him blow someone's brains out. Secondly, he had a gun and I was unarmed. If I'd gone any easier, I might not be standing here right now."

They continue yammering questions but I've had enough.

"If you'll excuse me now, I have to get my daughter to soccer, and we would appreciate you leaving us alone from this point forward. Thank you."

I get in the car and then it gets very awkward. The damn car won't start. I keep turning the engine over but it's not sparking to life. The car is sounding like a dying animal on its last gasp of breath. Meanwhile, the cameras are still rolling and Addie is sinking further and further down into her seat, saying, "This is so embarrassing!" After a couple of minutes, I realize that the car isn't going anywhere and I'm sitting there trying to work out what to do. The camera crews are still filming but the reporters are all quiet now. It's a strange frozen tableau: they're all just standing around the car, looking at us and we're staring back at them. Finally, one reporter leans down and knocks gently on my window. She's got a CNN logo on her shirt. I wind the window down a bit and she gives me a sympathetic smile.

"Would you guys like a lift?"

Fifteen minutes later Addie and I are at the soccer ground. The reporter and her camera operator were actually pleasant, down-to-earth people and we had a very civilized discussion on the trip here. She had obviously wanted a little more background information on me, and I guess I relented a little and answered a few more questions. She was intrigued by my Australian accent and seemed to want to paint me as some kind of "Mad Max" tough guy, but I assured her I was a very ordinary guy. In the end, they dropped us off and she gave me her card, although I'm not sure what I would ever want it for.

"I think she likes you, Dad," Addie says as we walk toward the field her team has been allocated.

"Don't be silly. She's a reporter. It's her job to make you feel like she likes you."

Addie gives me a weird look and shakes her head.

"You're not very good at this stuff, are you?"

"What stuff?"

"Girl-boy stuff."

"Don't be ridiculous. There wasn't any girl-boy stuff going on."

"Ooooooh yes there was! I'm a girl and I'm telling you she was giving off signals like it was the fourth of July!"

"Really?"

"Yes! Really! You're terrible at this, Dad! You need help."

"That might be true if I was actually trying to find a girlfriend, which I'm not. So, no help is required, thank you very much."

"OK, but don't blame me when you end up a wizened, lonely old man, eating cat food and wearing slippers all day and smelling of urine."

"It's a deal. I definitely won't blame you."

The game gets under way shortly after, and I spend my time trying to watch Addie play while being surreptitiously chased up and down the sideline by the two predatory single moms. Both belong to the yummy mommy club, with bottled blonde hair and expensive figures that have obviously been shaped by many hours at the gym. Where are all those reporters when I need them? Half-time comes and I realize we left the oranges on the back seat of the dead Subaru. Fortunately, two parents are rostered on for oranges each week, so at least the players get one quarter to suck on each. I get disappointed looks from most of the parents, except for the two voracious single moms, both of whom smother me with sympathy and offer to give us a ride home. If I'm lucky they might come to actual blows over who gets to take us home. That could be quite entertaining.

The second half gets underway and we concede a quick goal. We're three down now and I've given up hope of a first win for the season. Addie is without doubt the best player on the team and I've got no idea why the coach has stuck her in the backs. With five minutes to go she makes a break downfield and lines up a shot on goal. It's a screamer, heading like a bullet for the goal, but instead, it smashes into the face of a defender about five yards in front of her. The defender drops like a sack of potatoes and the game seems to come to a grinding halt. Players from both sides gather around the fallen girl, concern etched onto their faces. But not Addie. She regathers the ball, dribbles around the fallen girl and blasts the ball into the back of the net. That's my girl! The other team object, claiming that the game had been stopped, but the ref explains that she hadn't blown a stop to the game, so the goal stands. Parents from the other team are clearly unhappy, and even some from our side are feeling a little awkward about it, but I'm proud of Addie. It's what I've taught her: play to the whistle and never give up.

We get a lift home from yummy mommy number one, and during the ride we get invited to dinner that night; 'just pizza and a cozy movie night'. Fortunately, Addie and I both have other plans, so we decline graciously. As YM1 drives away, Addie comments,

"Please, tell me you picked up on those signals, Dad."

"Yep. Picked up those signals, loud and clear. You see? I'm not as stupid as I look."

"I wouldn't go that far," she says condescendingly. "Even a blind and deaf mute could have picked up those vibes. She was radiating signals like a heat-seeking missile!"

Fortunately, by the time we return home, the press have all disappeared. My brief interview with them must have satisfied their appetite. Hopefully, they'll move on to the next exciting story now and leave us alone.

We get home and Addie dives into the shower to wash the mud off and start getting ready for a sleepover at her friend's. A bunch of girls from school are getting together to watch movies and talk about boys and eat junk food all night. I can't work out why they call it a sleepover.

I pick my phone up from where I'd left it on the kitchen bench and start deleting all the missed calls and messages from reporters. One voicemail message catches my eye, and I hit play.

"Hello Mr. Targett. It's Detective Abrams. Give me a call. You've got my number."

I decide I'll call him sometime tomorrow.

By 6:00 pm I've washed two loads of clothes, cleaned the bathroom and kitchen, and ordered next week's groceries online. Addie and I head out at the same time and I wait with her for a few minutes on the sidewalk outside our front door until her lift pulls up. She piles into the back seat and is immediately caught up in exuberant girl-talk with one of her friends. I say a brief thank you to the dad who is driving them. He's aware of our car situation and says it's no trouble to drop Addie home tomorrow.

It's only two miles to Karl and Billie's and it's a nice night for a walk. By the time I get there I'm feeling hungry and I can smell barbecue ribs cooking as I knock on the front door. Billie answers and gives me a kiss and a warm embrace. She's a young Meg Ryan look-alike and tonight she looks as gorgeous as ever.

"Karl's out the back, incinerating the ribs. You might need to save them."

I've known Karl and Billie for nearly sixteen years. We met at the Joint Forces Training Base, Los Alamitos. Karl was the Specialist Weapons Instructor and I was the Close Combat Instructor. We clicked right from the start and kept in close contact after I was discharged five years ago and moved to Santa Clara. Karl was discharged just eighteen months ago and moved up here as well, to take over the family gun shop and shooting range after his father's sudden death.

I head out to the back deck and Karl and I exchange a bro hug. He hands me a twist-top bottle of soda water and he cracks open another Budweiser. I stopped drinking five years ago. We clink bottles and take a swig.

"I saw the video, dude. Very impressive."

"Not perfect, though," I say. "The elbow strike was meant for his temple. I misjudged his forward motion."

"Still. It did the job. Exit one bad guy."

We clink bottles again.

"It looked like either a Glock 26 or a Springfield XD-M. The video wasn't super clear," he says.

"XD-M," I reply. "And by the extent of the splatter pattern, I'd say it was loaded with 147 grain hollow points."

We talk guns for a while and he tells me it's been too long since I used up some rounds at his range. We decide to try and work out a time to shoot together there soon.

Over dinner, Billie asks how my self-defense classes are going, and I give them a brief run down.

"You're a good man, John, giving up your time like that for free," says Billie.

"No, I'm not really. You both know why I do it."

They nod, and there is a moment's awkward silence.

"It wasn't your fault, John," says Karl.

"Really? I'm a self-defense expert and I never even taught my own wife."

"That's not exactly true. You tried, but she wasn't interested."

"I should have tried harder."

They decide not to push the point any further and we move on to safer topics. Half an hour later, over coffee and dessert, Billie broaches another topic.

"I was nearly very naughty tonight, John."

I raise my eyebrows at her, enquiringly.

"I nearly invited someone else to dinner."

"I presume you are referring to someone of the opposite gender?"

"There is absolutely no doubt whatsoever that she's of the opposite gender," says Karl with a wink and a leer, which he instantly regrets. As Karl rubs his arm in mock pain, Billie continues.

"She's absolutely lovely, John. She's smart, and witty. And yes, as my lecherous husband has correctly pointed out, she's very pleasing to the eye as well."

"So what's wrong with her? Why is she single? Is she missing a leg? Does she froth at the mouth and howl at the moon?"

"She's divorced. Two years ago. Hubby was a complete bastard. She's got no children and has a good job and ... well ...I think you would both get on brilliantly. I can picture you two together so easily."

"Terrific. Just hold onto that picture, if it makes you feel any better."

"Dude, you can't stay single forever, surely?" says Karl. "You must be ... I don't know ... you must get lonely sometimes."

I sigh.

"Yeah. I do. And when I meet the right person, I'll know. I

just haven't met her yet. And I'm still not sure I'm ready to get back in the saddle."

"Giddy up, bro," says Karl with a suggestive wink, for which he receives another thump on the arm.

A little after 10:30 pm I say goodbye and walk home, enjoying the cool night air and the solitude, wondering if everyone else is right about me. Addie and Karl and Billie all seem to think I should be dating again by now. Maybe they're right. Maybe I should be. But I can't help feeling like there's something broken inside me, and it's never going to get fixed.

5

———

I like Sundays. I have a routine that's comfortable and familiar. By 8:00 am, I'm back from my run, showered and changed. I head downstairs and walk next door to the Beanstalk. Costa spots me immediately. He's there seven mornings a week, without fail.

"Mr. John! Good morning to you! What can I get for you today?"

"Skinny cap with vanilla syrup, thanks Costa."

"Ah. Good choice! Good choice!"

There's no one in line so he quickly starts making me my usual long black.

"You are a hero, Mr. John! You are all over the TV!"

"I was just in the right place at the right time."

"You are a lethal weapon, eh? The best of the best?" he says, making ridiculous imitations of karate chops.

"Not really. The guy had no training. It wasn't a real contest."

He hands me the long black and I take a sip.

"How is it?"

"The best you've ever made, Costa."

"Ah! I thought so! I'll put it on your tab. Have a good day, Mr. John."

"You too, Costa."

A minute later I unlock the door to my office. The writing on my shop front window says, 'Targett Investigations: Professional, Domestic and Corporate Investigation'. Sunday is my day for catching up with paperwork, so I sit at my desk and call up my current and outstanding case files. Private investigation isn't the glamorous job that many people think it to be. The majority of my cases are for insurance companies, wanting me to verify workers' compensation claims. I've lost count of the number of people with 'serious back injuries' whom I've photographed doing heavy work around their home or even playing contact sport on weekends. Insurance companies love me.

The remainder of my work is domestic: mainly people wanting to know if their partner is having an affair. Occasionally I get a missing person's case or something a little more interesting, but the majority of my time is spent sitting in my car with a camera, waiting to get documentary evidence of some kind of indiscretion.

I call up the file for the 7-Eleven shop owner. I'm not sure if I'll get paid for that job, as I was only there for a couple of hours and now the employee certainly won't be doing any more smoking. I quickly draft an invoice for my time and email it to the owner, doubting that I will ever see any money from him. A couple of insurance companies are late paying my bill, so I send them a reminder. I've only got one active case at the moment; a woman who thinks her boyfriend is cheating on her. I'll need to get the car fixed ASAP, so I can get on the case.

I hear the front foyer door creak open and a moment later a shabbily dressed, overweight man walks through my office door.

"Detective Abrams," I say, somewhat surprised to see him.

"Mr. Targett," he replies, nodding his head.

He walks in and looks around, taking in the dated appearance of the décor and the tired looking furniture.

"It's a cozy little office you've got here."

"It's all I need. One day I might get around to sprucing it up a bit, but most people aren't interested in whether I'm featured in a home décor magazine."

He doesn't say anything, just nods.

"Can I get you a tea or coffee?"

"No. I'm good."

"In that case, what can I do for you? Do you usually work on a Sunday?"

"No. It's my day off. But what can I say? I've got no life." He smiles wistfully. "You didn't return my call."

"Sorry. I switched the phone off for a while yesterday. I was getting bombarded by news vultures. What did you want?"

"Just this," he says, holding out an official looking document that he's had in his hand. "It's a statement, transcribed from our interview with you on Friday night. We just need you to check it and sign it, so we can expedite proceedings against the scumbag."

I take the document.

"Always happy to help nail a scumbag."

He sits in the padded chair opposite my desk as I read through the transcript.

"Do you mind if I make a couple of alterations?" I ask when I've finished.

"Go ahead. Just initial in the margin."

I make a few changes, initial, then sign at the bottom and hand it back.

"Done," I say happily. "Exit one scumbag."

"Nice work, by the way," Abrams says as he puts the paper on the floor beside his chair. "I saw the CCTV as well as the YouTube video. Very impressive."

"Thanks. It wasn't perfect, but it got the job done."

He gives me a curious look for a moment.

"You're an enigma."

"How so?"

"You're a doctor."

"Not a medical doctor."

He takes a dog-eared, stained notebook out of his top pocket and flips it open.

"PhD in English Literature from Stanford University."

"That's correct."

He shakes his head.

"I don't get it."

"What's there to get? I had a change of career."

"What happened?"

"My daughter happened."

He regards me with a puzzled expression for a few moments.

"You know, I might take you up on that coffee after all. That's if it's still on offer."

"Sure. It's only instant, unless you want to grab one next door?"

"Instant will be fine. White with three sugars please."

A few minutes later I'm back with his coffee and he starts with the questions again.

"So what exactly happened with your daughter?"

"Is this relevant to your investigation?" I ask.

"Not really. So you don't have to answer. I'm just curious."

I look at him and sense something. Loneliness? Disillusionment? Weariness? I can't quite put my finger on it, but somehow I feel comfortable talking with him.

"I'd just completed an honors degree and was about to start my doctorate when Jessie and I got married. We'd been dating for two years before that. We'd met at college and by the time we got married she'd graduated and was working full-time as a librarian. It was our shared love of literature that drew us together in the first place."

I take a sip of the last dregs of my own coffee and Abrams stays silent, absorbing my story.

"We lived on Jessie's meagre salary while I worked on my doctorate. We were poor but happy. Then, two years into my thesis, she fell pregnant with Addison. We decided that I'd need to get a full-time job and finish my thesis part time. For six months I applied to every newspaper and magazine I could think of, hoping to get a gig as a journalist, but I kept getting knocked back. Then one day, out of the blue, an army officer walked into the self-defense class that I ran on campus."

"A free class?" asks Abrams.

"No, I wasn't as generous back then. I charged a little; not much. We needed the money."

Abrams glances at his notes again.

"You'd been a state and national mixed martial arts champion, several years in a row, in your late teens and early twenties."

"Yes. I started learning when I was fourteen. I was a wimp who was getting bullied at school and I wanted it to stop. It turns out I had a natural ability."

"So what happened with this army officer?"

"He was a colonel from the army recruiting department. I don't know how he found out about me, but he watched me run the class and then, afterward, he offered me a job: join the army and train elite soldiers in unarmed combat. The pay they were offering was exceptional. It was a no-brainer. I did fourteen weeks officer training, graduated as a second lieutenant, and was immediately posted to the Joint Forces Training Base in Los Alamitos. We lived there for ten years and loved every minute. I ended up a first lieutenant. I finished my doctorate in my sixth year there, but I've never really used it since."

Abrams is silent for a few moments, then gives me a piercing stare.

"I know what happened then."

"It doesn't surprise me."

"I got hold of your wife's case file from the LA Police Department."

I merely nod, feeling my stomach clench and my heart start pounding. I still can't think about it without reliving the heart-wrenching emotions of that night. Abrams glances at his notebook again.

"Attacked and strangled while jogging through El Dorado Park at around 9:00 pm."

I merely nod. There's a lump in my throat now.

"The case is still open. You were a suspect initially, weren't you?"

"Yes. You know the stats. Three quarters of all murders are committed by the spouse or a close acquaintance."

"And there was the issue of the insurance money."

"Yes. Jessie had only just taken the policy out. It looked very suspicious."

"But you were cleared."

"Yes. I was on a skype call at the time of the murder; at home looking after Addie while Jessie went for a run to blow off some cobwebs. I didn't know she'd gone to El Dorado, though. I'd always told her to stay on base if she was running after dark."

Abrams takes another sip of coffee.

"Why did you leave the army if you loved it so much?"

"I knew I couldn't keep doing it and look after my daughter properly at the same time. I needed something with more flexible hours. Plus, I wanted to move back here to the Santa Clara area. I was hoping to get a job at the University. This building came up for sale at just the right time. I bought it outright with the insurance money."

"So why private investigation?"

"I don't have a good answer to that, really. I kind of just drifted into it. The coffee shop was giving me a passive rental income, so I didn't need to work full time. I just wanted to do something that had flexible hours and would allow me to be here for Addie when she needs me. I pick and choose my cases. I occasionally also write a book review for a couple of magazines, which brings in a few dollars."

Abrams nods.

"Well, you certainly are one strange mixture, Doc."

"There's no need to call me 'Doc'."

"It's what you are. People should be recognized for what they've done and for who they are. Which brings me to the other reason I'm here." He pauses for a moment, gathering his thoughts.

"The scumbag you hammered is a member of a gang that operates in the area. Robberies, assaults, murders; that kind of thing. They don't take kindly to one of their own being arrested, and they especially don't appreciate it when a gang member is beaten up. Your name is now all over the news. They know who you are and, by now, they probably know where you live. I think you should take precautions."

"What kind of precautions?"

"Do you have a gun?"

"A couple."

"Have you got a Concealed Weapons Permit?"

"No."

"I'll email you an application. Fill it in and email it back to me. I'll get it approved within 24 hours. In the meantime, I'd be extra vigilant if I were you. In fact, if I were you, I'd start carrying a gun around straight away, without waiting for the permit." He fixes me with a penetrating stare. "But that's just me. I'm a non-conformist. As a policeman, I wouldn't dare suggest that you break the law in that way."

"Of course not," I agree.

"Good. I'm glad we understand each other, Doc."

He stands and hobbles toward the door.

"Oh, and by the way," he says turning back to me. "Don't let my partner get under your skin. Rosario gets under my skin enough for the both of us."

He nods and walks out the front door, leaving me with a lot to think about.

6

Monday mornings are always interesting in our household. Two days' absence from the 'repressive educational regime' and its 'intolerable fascist rules' tend to give my fledgling adult a taste of freedom, and she is usually extremely reluctant to submit herself once more to its 'cruel and unreasonable expectations'. I usually counter these kinds of philosophical objections with profound counter-arguments such as, 'suck it up, princess' or the always-handy, 'get your butt out of bed and stop whining'. This morning I go for the ageless, 'we all have to do things we don't like', which is always guaranteed to elicit a groan and a roll of the eyes.

Right now she's sitting at the kitchen bench in a onesie eating Froot Loops, which is the only breakfast cereal she eats. This is clearly a reflection of my poor parenting and for some strange reason, I choose today to challenge this particular culinary habit.

"You do realize, don't you, that actual fruit hasn't come within several miles of that cereal?"

"Good. That must be why it tastes so nice."

Ignoring her, I plow on.

"In fact, the term 'cereal' is a complete misnomer. Cereal implies that the product contains a significant percentage of grains and other plant-based products. The amount of actual grains in this whole box would probably barely fill a thimble."

"Good. None of those nasty pesticides used by farmers."

"Yes," I agree sarcastically. "And none of those nasty natural products like wheat or barley or rye. Just pure, unadulterated artificial colors, artificial flavors, artificial sweeteners, emulsifiers, sugar and cancer producing fatty acids. Do you know that when cockroaches eat this stuff they glow in the dark for a week?"

"The problem with you Millennials," she says as she stuffs another spoonful of colored poison into her mouth, "is that you're all obsessed with living a long life. Us Gen Z's have accepted the fact that humanity is going to blow itself up one day soon, so we just decide to enjoy ourselves in the short time that we have left."

She blows me a cheeky kiss as she gets up and runs to the bathroom to clean her teeth.

"Don't worry about rinsing your bowl," I call after her. "I can do that for you. I've got this. Truly, don't worry yourself about it at all. I'm here to help."

"I know," she says, sticking her head back out through the bathroom doorway. "That's why they pay you the big bucks. I'm just a helpless little girl."

Fifteen minutes later she flies out of her bedroom with her backpack over her shoulder and both hands engaged in putting her barely-brushed hair up into a ponytail. As she runs down the stairs on her way to the bus stop, she yells,

"'Bye Dad. Love you."

"Love you, too, sweetie."

Peace descends like the calm after a tornado, but with slightly less damage.

I spend a few minutes picking up various pieces of Addie's

clothing which have been strewn across most rooms of our apartment and then I head downstairs. I ask Costa for a flat white with almond milk and a few minutes later I'm walking out of the Beanstalk with a steaming cup of strong black coffee. I walk two blocks north and end up in the front office of Charlie's Auto Repairs. I could have tried phoning, but I know from experience that they rarely answer their phones until after midday.

"Top of the mornin' to ya, Mr. Targett," says Terry, who has been the owner of the business for over thirty years and has absolutely no idea who Charlie is or was. None of his employees do, either.

"Morning, Terry."

You really know you've got a complete bomb of a car when you and the local mechanic are on such familiar terms. Terry is in his early 60s; short and nuggety, with a gray-stubbled chin and an almost completely bald dome.

"I've got a bit of a problem with my car again."

"Is that so? I'm sorry to be hearin' that," he says in his broad Irish accent.

I'm quite sure he's not sorry at all. I've probably paid for his grandkid's private school fees for the last five years.

"The thing is, it won't even start this time. Do you think you could send someone down to have a look at it?"

"No trouble! No trouble at all! In fact, I'll do even better than that. I'll send Sean down with the tow truck and he'll pick it up and bring it back here. You leave it with us, Mr. Targett. We'll get to the bottom of it, for sure!"

I leave a few minutes later, after eliciting a promise that he won't do any work on the ageing wreck without giving me an estimate first. I've got a feeling that it might be almost time to upgrade to a car that doesn't have a cassette deck.

I walk back toward the office, enjoying the morning sunshine and sipping my coffee. I unlock my office door and

I'm almost at my desk when I freeze, with my coffee cup halfway to my lips. There's someone in the back storeroom. Or maybe it's the kitchen – I'm not sure. I'm perfectly still now, holding my breath, every sense supercharged. There it is again! A shuffle of feet and a rustle of material. Then the sound of someone exhaling as though they are lifting or moving something.

I move quietly to the desk and place my cup on it. I gently slide open the bottom drawer, lift my Glock 26 out and begin to move toward the curtain into the hallway. There's more rustling and feet shuffling. It's definitely coming from the back storeroom. I peak through the curtain. Nothing. With my pistol in a two-handed grip I step into the short hallway and quickly scan the kitchen. It's empty. There are four more steps to the end of the hallway where it opens into the storeroom. I take the steps extremely slowly, with my legs wide apart to avoid fabric rustle from my pants. As I reach the end I quickly step into the room and swing my gun around and center it squarely on his torso. He's bending over, with his back to me.

"Hands in the air and straighten up, nice and slow."

But he does neither. He cranes his neck around toward me and speaks in a high voice.

"Hi. You must be John Targett."

It turns out the he is a she.

"Who the hell are you?"

She turns back to what she was doing before, which was rummaging through a backpack. There's a bedroll and sleeping bag laid out on the floor along the right-hand wall, with a pair of discarded black sneakers beside it.

"Where is it? I'm sure I packed it," she says, as she continues searching with her back to me.

"Get your hands in the air so I can see them."

"Well that would hardly be fair. You've probably already had your breakfast and I'm starving. Ah here it is!"

She straightens up holding a green plastic breakfast bowl and a spoon. She turns and pads past me in bare feet, leaving me standing in the storeroom alone, still holding my gun. As she walks into the kitchen, she calls back to me.

"I'm going to use the last of your milk, by the way. You'll need to get some more."

I walk to the doorway of the kitchen and watch her tip raw muesli – a healthy version of granola – from a packet into her bowl. Where did the muesli come from? Where did she come from? What's going on here? I seem to have woken up in some kind of alternate reality.

"Um ...," I say drawing on my impressive reservoir of verbal skills.

"I'm Quinn, by the way," she says as she drains the last of my milk into her bowl.

"Quinn," I repeat.

"Yep. I'm your new assistant."

"Assistant?"

"Do you often repeat what other people say?"

"How did you get in here?"

"Through the back door."

"But it was locked."

"Yeah, well, ..." she smirks. "It wasn't much of a challenge."

I look down the hall at the back door which has two locking mechanisms, one on the handle and a deadlock higher up. They are both currently in the locked position.

"Those are good locks!" I say, defending my defeated security measures.

"What can I say? I have skills."

She's sitting cross legged now on the far kitchen bench, eating muesli with her back to the wall. I realize by now that I'm probably not going to shoot her, so I slip the Glock into my pocket.

She's average height with a lean build and very short jet-black hair. Tight black jeans, black T shirt , black nail polish, black mascara. The only thing that isn't black is the small gold ring that pierces her left nostril. It's hard to tell her age, but I'm guessing early twenties.

"By the way, I love your accent," she says with a mouthful of muesli.

"So let me get this straight," I reply, ignoring her comment. "You broke into my premises, slept in my storeroom, used up all my milk and now you tell me you're my new assistant."

"Plus, I used the shower last night. The hot water isn't working, by the way."

"Look, I don't know who the hell you are ..."

"Quinn. I told you."

"OK, Quinn. Here's the thing ..."

"Very nice. That rhymes."

I push on, ignoring her flippancy.

"Firstly, I don't want an assistant. Secondly, I don't need an assistant. Thirdly, I can't afford an assistant. And fourthly, this is break and enter, and I could call the police."

"You don't want to do that. I'm here to help. Like I said, I have skills. Plus, you can definitely afford me. All I need is somewhere to sleep and a supply of food. This back area of your office is a perfect crash pad."

I'm struggling to find words. I don't think I've ever encountered someone quite so brazen.

"Look, if you're homeless, I can talk to some contacts I have in community housing – get you some accommodation in a share house and get you on welfare. I'm happy to help. But you can't stay here."

She puts the bowl down and wipes a dribble of milk from her chin.

"John, you're not getting it. I'm not homeless – at least not in the sense you mean. And I'm not a welfare case. I like to describe myself as a vocational sampler. In the three years since finishing university, I've gate-crashed three different types of jobs. The last one was a software development company in Silicon Valley."

"Did you break into their offices too?"

"Sure. Three times, until they finally gave in and let me work there. I even got a salary in the end."

"I don't get it. Why are you doing this?"

She shrugged.

"Because I don't know what I want to do when I grow up, basically. And I'm not really in a rush to grow up yet anyway. I want to try on a whole bunch of different lives until one seems to fit."

"And I'm your next experiment, am I?"

"I saw you on YouTube, and when I heard you were a PI living right here in the valley, well, it just seemed like a great opportunity."

"How old are you?"

"How old are *you*?" she countered.

"Thirty-nine."

"Actually, I already knew that. I'm twenty-four. And don't worry; I'm not gonna try to jump your bones. You're way too old for me, dude."

"Thank you. That's very considerate of you."

"You're welcome."

I sigh and shake my head. This is completely surreal. She seems to sense that I'm weakening.

"Give me a week. If, at the end of that, you don't think I'm going to be useful, I'll split and go somewhere else."

This is bizarre. I can't believe I'm even considering her offer. I stare at her for a moment, my thoughts in a whirl.

She jumps down from her perch on the bench, reaches into her pocket and pulls out a handful of bullets, holding them out to me.

"You might want to reload your pistol. They tend to work better with bullets in them."

I stare at the bullets as she places them into my hand and then look back up at her. She's smiling. There are moments in life when the future hinges on the smallest of decisions. An unexpected encounter that, if pursued, will spiral off into further unforeseen events. Somehow, I sense that this is one of those moments.

"Would you like a coffee?" I ask.

And that's how I came to have an assistant.

7

Quinn has gone to the supermarket, two blocks away, with one hundred dollars of my cash in her pocket. As she left, I briefly wondered if I would see her again, but then I remembered all her gear in the storeroom. I'm fairly confident she'll be back. While she's gone, the plumber I phoned on Saturday arrives and starts fiddling with the hot water system in the corner of the storeroom. He wanders back into my office ten minutes later telling me what's wrong with it. All I hear is, 'Blah, blah, money, blah, blah, money'. The short answer is it's not worth fixing and I need a new one. There are several options; 'Blah, blah, money, blah, blah, more money'. I choose what seems to be the cheapest option and give him the green light. He writes me out a quote and tells me that he'll be back tomorrow to install it. Great. Addie's going to really enjoy having another cold shower, tonight.

The plumber has barely left when I hear Sean, Terry's son, pull up out the back with his tow truck. I go out, give him the keys and watch while he loads my antiquated jalopy onto his tip tray and drives off with it. I am secretly hoping that a meteor or a satellite will fall from the sky on top of it and write it off so that I can claim the insurance.

I walk back inside to find Quinn unloading bags of groceries in the kitchen. I am pleasantly surprised. There isn't a single box of Froot Loops in sight. Just loads of fresh vegetables, fruit, nuts, legumes and other stuff that I can't accurately name. It looks as though she has emptied out the entire health food aisle.

"You're a healthy eater," I observe.

"Pescatarian. Vegetables and fish, but no red meat."

"I should get you to talk to my daughter. She's convinced that anything natural is going to kill her."

I mention the hot water situation and Quinn asks to see the quote from the plumber. She reads it, frowning, while eating an apple, then she walks to the spare desk which she has now commandeered as her own, flips open her laptop and starts typing.

"If you need my Wi-Fi password ..."

"No need. I hacked it last night. Your security is pathetic, by the way. I'll set up a new security system with a VPN and fire-wall for you today."

"Right," I say, nonplussed.

She spends ten minutes furiously typing and clicking, then a further ten minutes on three different phone calls, using her mobile. Finally, she phones the original plumber, introducing herself as 'Mr. Targett's personal assistant' and negotiates the installation of a bigger, better hot water system for $85 less.

"Wow," I say, as she finally leans back with a satisfied smile on her face. "I'm glad I don't have to negotiate with you."

"What do you mean? You already did this morning, and you lost."

"Mm. I guess I did. What was your degree at university, personal assertiveness?"

"Computer Science."

"Are you any good?"

She puts her head down for a while, typing and clicking furiously. I think she's decided to ignore my question, but a few moments later my own laptop pings and my screen comes to life, revealing a message in a big, bold font that dominates almost the entire screen. It reads, 'YES. I'M VERY GOOD!' There are little animated emojis of fireworks exploding and champagne bottles popping all around the outside of the text.

"Like I said, I have skills."

"OK ... that's ... a bit frightening. You just did that?"

"No. I actually hacked your computer last night. I wanted to find out about you. I needed to know that I can trust you. I don't like discovering skeletons in the closet further down the track."

"There's nothing hiding in my closet."

"No, there isn't. Which is why I'm still here. You're as clean as a whistle. So clean, in fact, you're positively boring."

"Thanks."

"Don't mention it."

"I just did."

"Well don't mention it again."

"Are all our conversations going to be this quirky?" I ask.

"I hope so. It'll make life interesting."

The phone rings. It's Terry. I glance at the clock on the wall. 1:30 pm. Terry has discovered his telephone again. He informs me of a list of things that are problematic: blah, blah, money, blah, blah, money, blah, blah, lots of money. This is turning out to be a very expensive day.

"I'll be honest with ya, Mr. Targett," he says in his rich Irish brogue, "if it was a horse, I'd take it down to the back paddock and shoot it."

"Well, let's pretend it's a car for the moment. What do you suggest?"

"Pretty much the same. I'd be sellin' it to a spare parts yard, if it were mine. Don't get me wrong, I'll fix it if you want me to, but I reckon you'll be throwin' good money after bad."

He offers to buy it for $500 and I tell him I'll think about it. Quinn has been listening to my side of the phone conversation and has followed the basic gist of it. When I hang up, she's already typing and clicking furiously. She tells me to leave it with her for a while and she'll see if she can get a better offer. I decide to head upstairs for a bite of lunch.

It's a strange feeling leaving my office in the hands of a complete stranger, but as the only thing of any real value is still in my pocket, reloaded with bullets, I figure I haven't got much to lose. As I fix my lunch, I puzzle over how I missed noticing the lighter weight of the Glock without its bullets. I guess in moments of perceived extreme threat, the brain has a way of focusing all of your senses on that one threat, to the exclusion of almost everything else. At least that's what I'm telling myself, otherwise I'm really losing my edge.

After lunch, Quinn informs me she's found a spare parts yard that will pick the car up from the workshop and pay me $800 for my trouble. I tell her to accept the deal. While she's on the phone to them, I walk back to Terry's / Charlie's (he really should change his sign) and retrieve my junk from the car's interior. I toss most of it in Terry's dumpster – old road maps, logbooks, a broken umbrella, half a dozen apple cores, the bag of quartered oranges which I had forgotten about and numerous takeout food wrappers from my surveillance jobs. The only items I retain are my mobile phone holder, a charger, some indigestion tablets and a missing pair of Addie's soccer socks. As I walk back to the office, I try not to feel sorry for Terry's grandchildren; they're going to need a new benefactor now that such a regular source of income has been erased.

After dumping my rescued possessions back home, I jump on a bus and spend the rest of the afternoon at several used car lots downtown, kicking tires and peering under hoods. I know almost nothing about cars, except for where to put the gas, but I can't help noticing that none of the cars has a cassette deck. I don't have a lot of cash to splash around, but I think I can stretch to $6,000. By the end of the afternoon, I've narrowed it down to either a 2004 Toyota Sienna or a 2005 Ford Escape. After test-driving them both, I still can't decide, so I head home to think about it overnight.

I've lost track of time and it's 6:20 pm by the time I get back. I'm hoping Addie hasn't filled up on junk food, as I was planning on making a tuna casserole. But as I walk into the downstairs foyer, I discover that a miracle has taken place in my absence.

8

———

"You're eating vegetables!"

I'm standing in the doorway to my office. Addie and Quinn are sitting together at Quinn's desk, talking and laughing and eating ... yes ... it definitely is a bowl of vegetables!

"Hi, Dad! Quinn and I made ratatouille. You ought to try some. It's amazing!"

I have to admit, it actually smells amazing.

"Um, sweetheart, you do realize that those are vegetables you are eating, right?"

"Yep."

"I mean, real vegetables, that used to be in the ground. The kind that farmers grow. Do you want me to get an ambulance standing by, just in case your body goes into toxic shock?"

"Ha, ha. Very funny."

"Is he always this sarcastic?" asks Quinn.

"Pretty much. It's a standard 'Dad thing'. I think there's a course they must all go to."

"There's some left in the casserole dish if you want," says Quinn. "That's if you can refrain from being overly sarcastic."

"I'll be on my best behavior," I pledge.

The ratatouille is delicious and we devour the rest between us. I wasn't even sure that the oven worked, but Quinn informs me that it works fine, and apparently there are all sorts of pots and pans in cupboards that I have never bothered to open.

Addie and Quinn seem to be engaged in a conversation that is verging on indecipherable to me, speaking about a rapper who is "dope", a hip hop artist who is "totally GOAT, no cap", a movie star who is "snatched", and someone in Addie's year at school who is "salty", which is apparently not a compliment. It's moments like this when I really feel my age.

I leave the girls watching video clips on Quinn's laptop while I take the dirty dishes upstairs to wash them. I must remember to get Quinn some detergent and a couple of dish towels tomorrow. As I listen to them laughing and talking downstairs, I am already grateful for Quinn's presence in our household. She's been here less than twenty-four hours and she's saved me hundreds of dollars, got Addie eating vegetables, and apparently, in my absence this afternoon, revamped my computer security system so that it is now virtually impenetrable. Best of all, she and Addie seem to be getting on like a house on fire. This could be really good for Addie. At least, I hope it will be good for Addie. I know almost nothing about Quinn. I will need to monitor things closely.

I'm mid-way through drying the dishes when my phone rings. Looking at the screen, I see the name, Mortimer Claymore: my father-in-law, or technically, ex-father-in-law. I let it ring out. We're not exactly on speaking terms. We haven't been, since Jessie's death. In fact, the breakdown in relationship started well before that. Mortimer and Jessie's mom, Katherine, had been bitterly disappointed when we moved to Los Alamitos, 380 miles from their family home in Palo Alto. Jessie was their only daughter and they missed her terribly. They had also never envisaged her marrying a soldier. Mort owned his own law firm and they had expected their daughter to marry someone in a respected profession. A soldier who taught other soldiers how to beat the crap out of people didn't exactly rate on their social acceptability scale.

Thus, my relationship with them was already strained with both physical and social distance when Jessie was killed. Her murder was the final straw in our relationship. In their minds, it was my fault. My fault because I'd taken her away. My fault because I'd failed to protect her. They initiated legal proceedings to take Addie from me. A twelve-month battle for full custody ensued. They claimed that life on an army base was no life for a little girl, and they mounted a persuasive argument that I could not possibly care for her adequately while holding down a full-time instructor's job. They also seized on the fact that I often had a couple of beers of an evening, and they claimed that I was a drunk and an unfit parent. Both claims were untrue and extraordinarily hurtful. It's why I haven't had a drink for five years; I don't want to give them an excuse to accuse me again.

My discharge from the army and the purchase of this building, with its passive income and the possibility of a more flexible work life for me, was what convinced the court that Addie should stay with me. Mort and Katherine were devastated and we've hardly spoken since. They Skype Addie regularly – I sometimes hear Addie chatting to them in her bedroom with her door closed – and they take her for a day's outing occasionally, as we are now living only a short drive from them. But the bitterness between us remains, and some of their hurtful accusations during the court battle can't be unsaid.

My phone pings, and there's a text message from Mort. 'Please answer your phone. I want to talk.' A minute later, the phone rings again and I reluctantly accept the call.

"Yes." I can't even bring myself to say his name.

"Thanks for taking the call, John."

Silence. I'm not going to make this easy for him.

"I saw what you did. How you captured that criminal. That was very brave."

"Uh huh."

"Look, John, I know things haven't been good between us, and that's partly my fault."

"*Partly* your fault? I'd say it's all your fault! I was never good enough for your daughter from day one, and you let me know that, very clearly."

"I'm sorry you feel that way."

"Don't put this back on me, Mort! I'm not some insecure adolescent who is over-reacting. You and your team of solicitors made your opinion of me very clear!"

"I regret the hostile approach we took during the court case. Things were said that ... well ... shouldn't have been said."

"You're damn right they shouldn't have been said, because they aren't true! I'm a bloody good father, and she's a hell of a lot better off with me than she would have been with you!"

There was silence between us again.

"Look, I didn't call to pick a fight."

"Then why did you call?"

"I saw the TV footage on CNN of your car not starting."

"So?"

"I'm worried for you both. For Addison especially. You can't keep patching up that heap of junk. You need something reliable."

"There's no need for you to worry, the car's been fixed."

"Really? Where is it now?"

"Parked out the back, where it always is," I lied. "Running like a dream again."

"No it's not. I was just around there."

"You were ... what do you mean?"

"Listen John. Katherine and I are both retired now and, to be honest, I'm not up to driving a big SUV around anymore. We've just bought a brand-new Audi coupe. Drove it home yesterday. The Land Cruiser is just going to sit in our garage untouched. We want you to have it."

I'm speechless. Part of me is wondering whether this is a ploy to try to worm their way back into my good books in order to gain more access to Addie.

"I appreciate the offer, but I won't accept."

"John, don't be foolish. We're doing this for Addison. Please let us help."

"Sorry, Mort, but no. I'm not going to accept your charity."

"It's too late. It's already done."

"What do you mean?"

"It's sitting in your parking lot right now. The keys are under the mat near your back door and the papers have all been signed over to you. It's yours."

"Well in that case, I'm driving it straight back over to your place."

"And I will drive it straight back to yours," he countered. "And I'll keep doing that until you swallow that damn pride of yours and accept it. I won't back down on this, John."

I can tell he's serious, but the last thing I want is to feel like I'm in his debt. I say nothing, thinking it through.

"John, please listen to me. Katherine and I are getting older, and as we age, we see that we've made some mistakes – some very hurtful mistakes. Hurtful to you and to Addison. And we're sorry. Please let us help."

Suddenly, I do feel sorry for him. Jessie was their only daughter and Addie is their only grandchild. Perhaps it is time to bury the hatchet, for Addie's sake as well as for theirs.

"Okay. Thank you, Mort. That's incredibly generous. And thank Katherine for me, too."

"I will. And thank you, John. We'll be in touch."

I get off the phone and walk around to the parking lot. The top-of-the-line Land Cruiser is only two years old and the engine is barely run in. I sit in the car for a few minutes, smelling the still-new leather seats and staring at the dash-board which resembles the instrument panel of a passenger jet. There's not a cassette deck in sight. I reflect on the extraordinary couple of days that I've had. Things are definitely starting to look up.

So, why do I get the feeling that this is the lull before the storm?

9

The storm hits just a few hours later. Not wind and rain, but bricks and bullets. I'm not a particularly deep sleeper and the sound of breaking glass brings me instantly awake. I look at the clock. 2:15 am. Then there is the distinctive sound of four gunshots in the street directly below, the bullets shattering more glass. The gun blasts echo into the distance, magnified by the empty streets in the early morning stillness. I roll onto the floor and grab the Glock from my nightstand drawer. Tires screech and an engine roars as a car speeds off, heading toward the downtown area. I run to the window but it's already out of my line of vision.

I run across the hall to Addie's bedroom and open the door. She's still sound asleep. Leaving her there, I head downstairs, treading cautiously. It could easily be a trap, with someone waiting for me to come charging down the stairs so they can calmly blow my head off. I move silently on bare feet, checking all the shadows. When I reach the glass office door at the bottom, I use the cover of the foyer wall and quickly glance through the door. There's someone in there. I glance around again, and see the person move to stand behind my desk against the far wall. I hear a desk drawer being opened furtively.

I pause for a moment and calculate the angles, then I burst into action. I reach around the door frame and switch the office lights on, leaving me in darkness in the foyer. Immediately, I dive to my left and do a sideways roll across the tiled floor of the foyer, ending up lying on my stomach with the pistol extended in front of me in a two-handed grip and my arms pointing through the open door directly at the figure behind my desk. Getting down low is the safest option in a situation like this, as gun-happy thugs with no military training will almost always stand and blaze away at chest height, leaving you a clear shot.

I've got a clear shot now, but I don't take it. It's Quinn. She's momentarily dazzled by the bright lights then ducks down behind the desk. Shit! I'd forgotten all about her. I almost shot her!

"Don't shoot! Don't shoot! It's me! It's Quinn!"

"Yeah, I can see that, now. I'll do you a deal: I won't shoot you if you don't shoot me."

"What the hell am I gonna shoot you with? My finger?" she yells, her voice betraying her fear.

I get up and walk over to her.

"Are you OK?" I ask, scanning the room as I do so.

"Holy crap!" she says, as she gets slowly to her feet. "What the hell just happened?"

"We've been paid a little visit."

"If that was a 'little' visit, I sure as hell don't want to be here when you get a big one."

She closes the desk drawer.

"I was looking for your gun. I was scared that someone might still be here."

"I took it upstairs," I explain. "I didn't want you mucking around with it again in case you shot your big toe off."

We scan around the office, checking the damage. The front window has been shot to pieces and there's a house brick in the middle of the threadbare office carpet. I pick it up and turn it over. '*Die pig!*' is scrawled in white paint. Most of the window is in pieces all over the floor, but parts of the top section are still hanging there. The sign writing on the window used to read, 'Targett Investigations', but now it simply reads, 'get … tiga'. I shake my head and smile. Maybe it's a secret message from the ghost of A.A. Milne.

There are three bullet holes in the back wall that separates the office from the kitchen, all at about head height. Looking back into the foyer, I can see that the glass door to the street is also shattered. That must have been the fourth bullet. It's probably buried in one of the steps.

"Oh my God, you're bleeding!"

I look down, and find that I am. My pajama shirt is sliced open on my left side and a fair amount of blood has now stained the whole side of my shirt and the top of my pajama pants. I must have rolled across some broken glass. I can also feel some small cuts on the soles of my feet where I've walked on broken glass.

"What are you smiling for?" she asks.

"I was just thinking that I'm glad it's not the middle of summer, otherwise I'd be standing here stark naked."

"You have to do something! You're bleeding badly."

I unbutton my shirt and find a deep gash across the side of my ribs.

"You need to go to the hospital!"

I shake my head.

"I'm not sitting in a waiting room for ten hours when I can sew it up myself."

"Are you kidding me?"

"It's no big deal. I've got an army issue field medical kit."

I bunch my shirt up and press it against my side, which

helps to push the two sides of the gash together and stem the bleeding for the moment. The medical kit is on the top shelf of one of the wall cupboards in the office kitchen. While Quinn fetches it, I phone the police and give a basic report of what's happened. As no one has been shot or injured, apart from my own self-inflicted wound. I'm informed that the boys in blue won't be rushing to get here.

"You may as well take your bedroll and sleeping bag upstairs and get some sleep," I tell Quinn. "I'll stay here and watch the place until the police get here."

"What about your wound? Don't you need help?"

"No, I'll be right. It'll give me something to do while I'm waiting."

After Quinn heads upstairs, I clean the wound with disinfectant and sew it up with a suture needle and silk surgical thread. I've seen people do it in the movies, and figure it can't be too difficult.

"Bloody hell!" I exclaim, as I push the first suture through. It hurts a lot more than I thought it would. I seriously consider going upstairs and getting a bottle of whisky that has sat untouched in the cupboard for the last five years. I decide to go ahead without it, but it takes me a few minutes to work up the courage to push the next suture through. In the end, it takes seven sutures to close the wound, and by the time I've finished I'm covered in sweat and I've sworn like a trooper for nearly twenty minutes. So much for my abhorrence of bad language.

I dab the wound with more antiseptic and then stick a bandage over it. It's throbbing like hell now and it doesn't look particularly neat, but I've probably just saved myself half a day at the hospital. There are some other smaller cuts on both forearms that I spend a few minutes cleaning up, as well as some small cuts on the soles of my feet. As I'm packing up the medical kit, I see a small vial of local anesthetic and a couple of syringes in sealed containers. Great! Note to self: check entire contents of field med kit next time!

I sweep some of the glass away from the foot of the stairs and quickly head upstairs to put on some warm clothes and shoes, as there is a cool breeze coming through the smashed window now. Quinn is sound asleep on the lounge room floor, so I'm careful not to wake her.

I spend the next three hours sitting in my drafty office, waiting for the police to arrive. By the time they get there I've got all my accounts in order, answered all my emails, and got to level three on Angry Birds 2. It's the first digital game I've played in about ten years and I'm feeling pretty happy with my achievement until I do a Google search and discover that it has over two thousand levels.

The sun is rising by the time a squad car finally arrives, and I can't help myself.

"Thank goodness you're here officers. You're just in time; they went that way," I say, sarcastically, pointing down the street.

They think I'm serious and explain politely that the offenders will be long gone by now. These guys have clearly fallen out of the stupid tree and hit several branches on the way down. They spend a few minutes checking the place out before deciding that I wasn't making it up when I phoned in a shooting. They call for a backup forensics team and take some photographs, telling me not to touch the brick as they will need to lift fingerprints from it. They disappear soon afterward, telling me not to clean up or move anything else until forensics has been.

An hour later – by which time I still haven't progressed past level three on Angry Birds – a forensics team of one turns up. He looks like a college student doing work experience and he confirms that they are, indeed, bullet holes in the wall. I tell him that this is a great relief, as I thought I had brick borers. On the positive side he is able to tell me what I'm doing wrong in Angry Birds, and within minutes I'm up to level four.

After taking a few more photographs and telling me that it's not possible to lift fingerprints from a brick, he leaves. He's probably got an early gym class to go to.

By now it's after 7:00, so I call a local glazier who promises to get the window and door re-glazed by the end of the day.

I can smell Costa's coffee now, so I head next door and order a strawberry milkshake with chocolate sprinkles. Costa makes me a strong black coffee and I spend the next ten minutes telling him of the night's excitement. He's obviously worried, not only for me and Addie, but also for his business. I'd like to assure him that it's not likely to happen again, but I can't. I honestly don't know.

10

Shortly after I get back from Costa's, Quinn comes downstairs, grabs a bowl of her muesli and sits at 'her' desk. I leave her to look after the office and keep out any curious passers-by while I go upstairs and get Addie organized for school. Tuesday mornings aren't as difficult as Mondays, as she has gym first up and she's got a crush on the teacher who is in his first year of teaching.

"Your hair looks nice, this morning," I comment as she devours her bowl of radioactive carbohydrate. "Got a hot date?"

She just rolls her eyes and shakes her head. Apparently, my comment is so lame it doesn't even warrant a response. I must be losing my touch.

Addie slept through the whole event last night, so I have to tell her what happened, trying to play it down so she doesn't freak out.

"So, is it gonna be safe to stay here tonight?" she asks, looking worried.

"I think so, sweetie. They weren't trying to hurt us, just scare us. They've done what they wanted to do and I don't think they'll be back." I wish I was as confident as I sound.

As a special treat, I drive her to school in our 'new' car. She's happy to be driven right up to the school gate in this car. If I ever drove her to school in the old jalopy, I had to drop her at least two blocks away, and even then, she wouldn't get out of the car if there were other students in sight.

By the time I get back to the office, the glazier is chipping away the last of the glass from the front window, and his apprentice is working on the front door. Quinn has a takeout coffee cup from the Beanstalk perched on her desk and is engrossed in something on her laptop.

"How's the coffee?" I ask.

"Great, but the big guy wouldn't let me pay for it. Says he'll just put it on your tab. Sorry."

"Costa." I inform her. "He's the owner. I told him about you this morning. Good luck trying to give him any money. There is no tab; he's just a really nice guy."

"He's certainly larger than life."

"What are you up to this morning?" I ask. But I've barely uttered the words when Detectives Abrams and Rosario step through the now completely empty window frame.

"Doing some redecorating, I see," says Rosario, looking around. "I like the holes in the wall. Very urban chic."

Abrams is a little more sympathetic.

"Sorry to hear about last night, Doc. Mind if we sit down?"

I point them to the two padded chairs on the other side of my desk, and Abrams continues.

"We're pretty sure we know who is responsible, although there is no proof, of course. The guy you beat up on Friday night is a member of a local gang. He's still not talking to us; not that that will hinder our prosecution. He's going away for a couple of decades, so you don't have to worry about him."

"But I do have to worry about his fellow-primates?"

"Unfortunately, yes. They call themselves the Eskimos."

"Not a very politically-correct name."

"No. Not that they care. It's a double-play on words. They see themselves as ultra-cool, plus we believe they're also involved in trafficking ice. You've probably seen their tags on older buildings and pavements in some of the backstreets around here. An igloo with a small arched doorway, but without the horizontal base line. In other words, two curved arches, with the smaller arch inside the larger one."

"Yeah. I've seen it."

"They're a Latino gang operating in the Santa Clara area. Fully-fledged gang members have both arches tattooed on the back of their neck. A fledgling member, called an Eski, only has one arch until they prove themselves by committing a worthy crime like armed robbery."

"Let me guess. The guy I hit was an Eski."

"Yes. He was hoping to earn his second arch. You should be thankful he wasn't a full-blown Eskimo, Doc, or you'd probably be dead by now. They're not quite as protective of their aspiring apprentices. In fact, they tend to regard them as expendable."

"So, do I have to worry about further attacks?"

"I'd like to say no, but I'm not confident. While they don't seem to give a crap for their apprentices, they're highly protective of their gang reputation. It might not be their last visit to you."

"Is there any way you can trace the car that was involved last night? What about CCTV?"

"We've already checked. It was driving without lights so we couldn't read the plates. Even if we could, it probably wouldn't do any good because the vehicle was almost certainly stolen."

"So, what do you suggest I do?"

"There's nothing much you can do, unfortunately."

"Maybe next time, you'll think twice before you race in and try to be a hero," says Rosario, referring to my capture of the gang member on Friday night. "Stick to taking photos of people doing gardening and leave law enforcement to the experts."

"You mean the experts who showed up after it was all over? The ones who hid behind their cars and were about to shoot me in the back? Those experts?"

She just gives me an icy stare that makes me want to check the back of her neck for tattoos.

"Look, we're all on the same side here," says Abrams. "We'll keep working the case from our end. If we make any progress, we'll be back in touch. In the meantime, I suggest you avoid going out late at night for the next couple of weeks."

"She's delightful," says Quinn, after they've left.

"Yes. I feel all warm and gooey whenever she's around," I agree.

"You should ask her out. She's probably a tiger in the sack."

"I picture her more as a black widow spider who eats her partners after copulation."

Quinn chuckles.

"I don't think it's safe for you to be here," I warn. "I think you should consider breaking into someone else's office and forcing yourself upon them."

She looks up from whatever she's doing on her laptop.

"No way. This is just getting interesting. Besides you need me."

"What exactly do I need you for?"

"This," she says pointing to her laptop. "I've tracked the car from last night."

"What? How did you do that?"

"I keep telling you, I've got skills. I've hacked into the city's CCTV system."

"How the hell did you do that?"

"Let's just say that I'm part of a certain online community that operates in the gray areas."

"How gray?"

"Dark gray."

"You're a hacker? Are you famous or something?"

"I have a reputation."

"What's your nickname?"

"Do I look stupid or something?"

"OK, but if you're involved in illegal online activity, I don't think I want you in my office."

She sits back in her chair and gives me a frank gaze.

"Look, dude, in the hacking community there are good guys and there are bad guys. I'm one of the good guys. The bad guys are only interested in anarchy and destruction. They get a kick out of it. But there are a lot of us who are simply convinced there is too much secrecy and incompetence in the digital world, and we enjoy helping people like you get the information you need."

She continues to stare at me, watching me wrestle with my conscience.

"Do you want my help, or not?"

"What have you found?"

"Is that a 'yes' to me helping you?"

"Yes. Thanks."

She brings her laptop over to my desk, along with her chair, and squeezes in beside me.

"Here is the car, running a red light on the corner, a few seconds before the shooting. Like the detective said, its lights are off and the plate is indistinguishable."

I look closely. It appears to be a dark-colored family station wagon of some kind.

"It doesn't appear on the CCTV footage from the camera at the next set of lights, so I figured it turned off before then. I spent some time tracking possible routes and picked it up again here, two blocks over."

An image of the same car appears on the screen.

"After that it was relatively easy to track. You can see that they turn the driving lights on here, and the plates are visible. They drive for another few miles and then I lose them in between these two cameras. Conveniently, there are no cross streets between those two cameras, so they had to have dumped the car in that stretch of road."

She calls up a different screen showing a vehicle registration paper.

"This is the rego for the car. It's registered to a Warren Blackall, and the address is smack bang in the middle of that section of road."

She calls up another screen.

"This is a picture of Warren. He's a middle-aged architect for a firm in San Jose, married with three kids. A respectable, boring citizen. I'm guessing that dear old Warren got up and drove to work this morning without realizing that his car had been borrowed overnight."

She flicks back to CCTV footage.

"A few minutes after the car disappeared from the footage, this car emerges from the street, heading back in the opposite direction. The only other vehicles for five minutes after that are two trucks and a motor-cycle."

She starts clicking quickly through CCTV images.

"I followed it back to here and lost it after this camera. It doesn't appear on any footage from surrounding cameras. I'm guessing it had to be parked within this circle; a radius of about five hundred yards. Significantly, there are very few houses in the area. It's a light industrial zone on the northern outskirts of Santa Clara. Mainly small industrial units and workshops."

"Wow! I'm impressed."

"Wait, there's more. This is who the vehicle is registered to. Antonio Sanchez."

A picture of a nasty-looking character pops up on the screen. It's a police mug shot. He's got a tattoo of an inverted cross in the middle of his forehead and a jagged scar down his left cheek.

"He's got a rap sheet as long as your arm. Done time inside

for armed robbery and attempted murder. This is his address. It's about three miles from the search area I circled. So I scanned the footage of a camera close to his house, in a direct line with where we lost the car. A bit after four this morning, the car drove past. I'm guessing he's going home after spending the rest of the night in that industrial area."

"Wow!" I repeat, in an impressive display of my wide vocabulary. "Why didn't you tell all this to the detectives when they were here?"

"Oh sure! That would have been really sensible. The black widow would have had me in cuffs in a flash for unlawful access of secure police security systems. No thank you!"

I sit back and try to work out what to do with the information.

"So, you think the gang might have some kind of base in that industrial area?" I ask.

"Or a drug lab. Or possibly both. Maybe in a factory unit or something."

I try to think what to do next.

"Our options are limited at the moment," I say, thinking out loud. "Even if we could get all this information to the police, it's circumstantial at best. There's nothing for them to act on."

"So, what do you want to do?" she asks.

"Can you keep monitoring the movements of that car? See if there's some kind of pattern? Maybe things will become clearer in a few days."

I just hope they don't become dangerously clear.

11

I sit pondering my predicament. My main concern is Addie. Should I arrange for her to stay somewhere else for a few days? I'm reluctant to ask Mort and Katherine to look after her, because it would only reinforce their view that Addie isn't safe living with me. Of course, at the moment they could actually have a point. Karl and Billie would take her in a heartbeat, as they are childless and they love Addie to bits. IVF didn't work for them. I put off making a decision for the moment.

By lunchtime, the window and door panes have both been replaced and the glazier leaves me his invoice. It's just as well I didn't fork out six grand for a car yesterday; the windows must be impregnated with diamond chips. I'm now thinking about my new Land Cruiser. The dark gray coloring is ideal for surveillance work, but I'll need to do something about the windows. Quinn offers to track down a window tinter for me and, after a couple of phone calls, finds someone who is able to come and do it this afternoon.

I'm about to suggest that we break for lunch, when a prospective client walks through the door.

"Is this the private investigator's office?"

"Yes. Sorry, we've just had our front window replaced and I haven't gotten around to getting a new sign."

I stand and hold out my hand.

"I'm John Targett."

He shakes my hand.

"Cory Wainwright."

"Please, sit down. What can I do for you?"

He sits and seems uncertain how to proceed. I'm immediately thinking; cheating partner. He looks about thirty. Dark curly hair and tanned skin. Medium build, medium height, medium everything. Nothing of particular significance about him at all."

"I ... um ... have an unusual problem."

"You've come to the right place. I specialize in unusual problems."

He hesitates some more, and I remain silent, allowing him to get his thoughts together. I notice that he's holding a small plastic shopping bag in his lap. Finally, he takes a deep breath and says something that, in my limited experience as a PI, I've never heard before.

"I don't think I'm me."

I blink.

"You don't think you're you?"

"Yes."

At this point, I'm trying to decide what branch of medical or social services I should be contacting to get this guy some psychiatric help.

"So, who do you think you are?" I'm thinking: Batman? Spiderman? Captain America?

"That's just it. I don't know."

"What makes you think you're not you?"

He takes another deep breath.

"Maybe if I explain from the beginning?"

"OK. I'm listening." But in my mind, I'm already filing Cory Wainwright under 'N' for nutcase.

"According to my birth certificate, my name is Cory Allan Wainwright, born twenty-nine years ago, on 14th September, in St Aidan's Private Hospital, San Jose. Here's a copy of the birth certificate."

He takes it out of the plastic bag and hands it to me. I examine it carefully. His parents are listed as Allan and Helen Wainwright.

"That all looks fine," I say.

"Yes. Now here is my baby book, issued by the baby health clinic that my mother started attending with me. The first entry is exactly one week after my birth, 21st September. My weight is listed as ten pounds two ounces."

He shows me the first page of the book and I see the entry for his weight.

"Uh huh. You were a big, healthy baby."

"Yes, apparently I was. Now, here is a photo of me, coincidentally dated the same day as that entry. It's taken in the lounge room of our family home. That's my mother holding me, and my older sister sitting beside us. She must have been seven at the time."

I take the photo. Cory was certainly a chubby baby. Turning it over, I see some faded writing which says, "Cory. 21st Sept.'

"OK," I say. "I don't see a problem with any of this."

"No. Not so far. But one of the things that has always intrigued me is why there are no photos of me in the hospital. There are photos of my sister on the day she was born. Lots of them, with Mom and Dad holding her and looking so proud. But there are none of me in the hospital."

I shrug. "It sometimes happens that second and third children don't have as many photos taken of them," I suggest.

"Yep, that's a reasonable theory, except that throughout the rest of my infancy, there are just as many baby photos of me as of my sister, Caroline. It's just the first week that's missing with me."

"Perhaps they just forgot to take photos at first." I am now trying to think of a way to terminate this conversation, because I'm quite sure this is a waste of my time.

"The other thing that's always puzzled me," he says, ignoring my comment, "is why my sister's baby book – her baby health record – was issued by the hospital, and contains a record of her birth weight, whereas my book was issued by the community baby clinic and starts a week after my birth. Plus, it has no mention of my birth weight."

I'm struggling to stay focused by now. I'm hungry and I just want Cory to leave so I can grab something to eat.

"Look, Cory, I don't think there's anything I can ..."

"Please, just hear me out," he pleads. "My father died ten years ago and my mother died last week. My sister and I have been clearing out their house, ready for sale, and I came across a small shoe box in the attic that had been taped up. I found some things inside it that shocked me."

Now he reaches into the plastic bag and takes out a photo. He hands it to me without saying anything. It's clearly a photo of his mother holding a baby while sitting up in a hospital bed. She has the look of a woman who has just given birth. I turn the photo over. It says, 'Cory Allan Wainwright', and his birthday is scribbled underneath. I turn the photo over again and I notice that a digital clock on her nightstand says 2:48 am.

"Look closely at the baby," he says. I notice he doesn't say 'look closely at me'.

The baby is scrawny. Clearly underweight. Nothing like the photo of the chubby baby dated just one week later.

"Look at the baby's left hand."

I look carefully. There is a large birthmark covering almost the entirety of the back of the baby's hand. My eyes quickly switch to Cory's left hand, which he is already holding out to me. We lock eyes for a moment.

"That's not me."

"No, it's not," I agree. I'm trying to think of an explanation. "Could your mother be holding someone else's baby for a moment? Perhaps the baby of another mother in a shared ward?"

"St Aidan's only has private rooms in the birthing unit and in its adjoining maternity ward. Besides, that's definitely my mother's writing on the back. She wouldn't have made a mistake identifying me in the photo."

"No. I suppose not."

"I also found this in the box."

He hands me a faded and yellowed baby book, issued by St Aidan's Private Hospital. The first page has Cory's name and date of birth on it. The book is blank – no records of immunizations or boosters or weights – except for a single entry on the first line. 'Birth Weight: 5lb 1oz'.

I look up and meet Cory's eyes again. He's got my full attention now, all thoughts of lunch gone.

"I'm sure you're aware, Mr. Targett, that babies can lose up to ten per cent of their birth weight during the first week. But no baby doubles its weight during that time. It just doesn't happen."

"No, they don't," I agree. "Have you been to the hospital to ask for your birth records?"

"Yes. When a baby is born all its birth details are entered into the birthing unit's digital birth register. Date, mother's name, baby's name, time of birth, weight, size, complications in the delivery, responsiveness, Apgar score, visible marks or abnormalities – a whole range of things. When they called up my record, all it contained was my name and my mother's name. Everything else was blank. The nurses were very apologetic and couldn't explain it."

We are both silent for a moment as I consider everything he's told me.

"How would you like me to help you, Mr. Wainwright?"

He fixes me with an intense gaze.

"I want you to find out who I really am and what happened back then."

12

———

"This is so exciting!" says Quinn, sitting cross-legged on her desk and eating a salad sandwich on sourdough that she's made from her own supplies. "This is exactly the sort of case I was hoping for when you hired me."

"Correction: I didn't 'hire you'. You broke into my office and demanded that I let you work for me. There's a significant difference."

"Well, if we're going to quibble, you did try to shoot me."

Ignoring her exaggeration, I ask, "How did you know how to disarm the gun, by the way?"

"I googled it."

"Of course you did."

I take a bite from my pastrami on rye that I bought from the deli down the road.

"Did you know that pastrami comes from the fatty flesh around the cow's navel?" she asks. "It's soaked in salty water for days while it's raw, then it's partially dried while still raw, and finally it's smoked. It contains more potentially dangerous bacteria than just about any other cut of meat."

"That must be why it tastes so nice," I say, taking another bite.

She screws up her face. "Anyway, as I was saying, this is really exciting!"

"Just don't get the wrong idea," I say. "Ninety five percent of investigative work is mind-numbing surveillance. Hours and hours of sitting on your ass, waiting for something to happen so you can get a photo and go home. Trust me, it's not usually this interesting. In fact, this is the first case like this I've ever had."

"You see! I've already brought you luck!"

"I must admit, you've been very helpful."

"Like I keep saying, I've ..."

"Got skills. Yes, I know. Speaking of which, your skills will certainly be useful for the first part of this investigation."

"What do you need me to do?"

"I want you to dig into those hospital records and see if there's anything that can give us a lead. Also, have a look at the baby health clinic's records for Cory. See if there's anything unusual there."

"Too easy. Anything else?"

"Yeah. I need help getting out of Level 4 on Angry Birds 2. What's the secret?"

"How long have you been on that level?"

"Since yesterday."

She gives me a sad look and shakes her head.

"Here's my advice: stick to golf, old man."

The rest of the afternoon passes quickly. I try to phone Cory's sister, using the phone number he gave me before he left, but it rings out. I don't leave a message. The car windows get tinted and I arrange for car insurance, which I really should have done yesterday. Quinn goes out for a while and I review my two other active cases. An insurance company I regularly do work for wants me to check up on a workers' compensation claim. A worker in an engineering plant in San Jose says he fell down some stairs at work. He's been off work for three months and has a medical certificate saying that he is unfit for work, citing chronic pain and limited mobility due to suspected nerve damage. He's supposedly in a back brace.

The second one is a classic cheating spouse case. A young woman suspects that her partner is having an affair on Thursday nights. He goes bowling with a mate every Thursday night and gets home very late. Twice recently she has smelt a woman's perfume on him when he returned home, and on one occasion she saw what looked like a hickey on the side of his neck. When she challenged him about it, he claimed it was a mosquito bite that he had been scratching and which had become slightly infected.

I decide to spend at least part of the day tomorrow on surveillance.

Addie arrives home a bit after four and by then I've decided that I need to move her somewhere safe for at least a couple of nights. I don't want Quinn here either; not until I'm confident that the danger has passed. I phone Karl and explain the situation and he is very happy to have the two girls stay with them for a few nights. He invites us all over for dinner.

As I get off the phone, Quinn walks in the door with a motorcycle helmet under her arm.

"I picked up my bike," she explains. "I loaned it to a friend for a few days."

"I'm surprised," I reply.

"That I ride a bike?"

"No. That you've got friends."

"You're hilarious."

Addie must have heard the bike pull up in the back parking lot, because she comes downstairs to check it out, and Quinn takes her out to show her. When they come back inside, I explain my plan to move them to Karl and Billie's for a few nights, and that's when the negotiations start.

Quinn says she'd prefer to stay here. I tell her that's not an option. She then says she'll couch-crash at a friend's house for a few nights. Addie complains that she doesn't want to go either. I tell her she doesn't have a choice. She says she doesn't want to feel like an orphan, staying by herself at Karl and Billie's and wants me to stay over there with her. I tell her I need to stay here to keep an eye on the place. She asks if she can stay at a friend's house. I tell her I don't want to impose on school friends and I certainly don't want to broadcast our problems to any more people than is absolutely necessary. Addie then pleads with Quinn to stay with her at Karl and Billie's. Quinn wants to know whether they are 'fascist uptight conservatives'. I assure her that they are very cool people. Finally, all parties are in agreement and I feel like the Secretary General of the United Nations who has just negotiated an international peace treaty.

A little before six, we head over to Karl and Billie's, with Quinn following on her bike. I know nothing about bikes but it has a classic look to it and Quinn tells me that it's an old Yamaha V-Star Cruiser that she picked up for a bargain price a few years ago.

Once introductions are made, dinner is a happy, boisterous affair, with banter flying around the table. Billie has cooked a vegetarian lasagna and a creamy potato bake in deference to Quinn's culinary preferences. Billie and Quinn are almost complete opposites in looks. Billie is the blond, green-eyed Meg Ryan type and Quinn has the dark featured, heavily made up gothic look. But in spirit, they are very similar – unconventional, slightly rebellious free-spirits – and they immediately hit it off.

"What made you want to give PI work a try?" Karl asks Quinn at one point.

"I enjoy solving puzzles and I like the idea of helping people."

"Do you have family?" This is a question I've been meaning to ask but haven't had the right opportunity.

She shrugs. "Various sets of foster parents spread around the state. The last ones weren't too bad." She thinks about it for a moment longer. "Actually, they were probably all OK. It was me who was the problem. I went through some pretty dark years."

"What about your natural parents?" asks Billie.

"No idea. I'm your classic foster child cliché: a drug addled mother who died when I was a toddler, and you can take your best guess as to which of her one-night stands was my father."

"Ouch," responds Billie. "That would have been tough."

"I've had my moments of wanting to kick the shit out of the world for dealing me a bad hand."

"But not anymore?"

"I finally realized that I'm not my past. I refuse to let my mother's poor choices poison my life as well."

A little later, Karl and I are sitting on the back deck together, having a drink. I've finally relented and I'm having a beer with him – my first drink in five years.

"Dude, are you sure you're gonna be OK over there by yourself tonight? Let me stay there with you."

"I'll be fine. Even if the bad guys come back and shoot the place up again, I'm not in any real danger. The angle of fire from the street is too steep to reach me in bed. All they can do is break more glass and redecorate the back wall downstairs. Besides, I think they've made their point. I doubt that they'll be back."

He tries to convince me to let him come over for the night and bring his own impressive arsenal of handguns, but I assure him that won't be necessary.

By the time I leave later that night, Quinn has cleaned up the hard drive on their computer and beefed up their digital security, and Addie and she are playing some weird interactive game on the game console that involves jumping all over the lounge room. Billie promises to get Addie to bed at a reasonable hour and Karl says he will drop her at school on his way to the gun shop tomorrow.

I head home to an empty apartment, thankful for good friends. But as I sit in my lounge room with the lights out, listening to the night sounds of the city, I feel lonelier than I have for a long time.

13

I must have fallen asleep on the lounge, because the next thing I know, the lounge room window is exploding inward and plaster is flying through the air from the bullets that are peppering the ceiling. I immediately recognize the distinctive sound of an M4 Carbine automatic rifle. At the same time I hear something that chills me to the bone.

"Dad! Dad!"

It's Addie's voice, followed immediately by her terrified screams.

Without thinking I am running down the stairs and I'm only halfway down when I hear the office window shatter, followed immediately by a violent explosion that rocks the whole building. A deadly blast of glass and shrapnel rips through the foyer below me, but I don't stop, because Addie is still screaming. It's coming from the street, not the office. The glass door to the street has been completely blown away and as I run through the opening onto the sidewalk outside, I see Addie being thrown into the back seat of a black SUV. The M4 is sticking out of the open front window and the person firing it has now spotted me. As he swings the rifle toward me, I realize that I've left my gun upstairs on the nightstand. I dive to the left as a hail of bullets rakes the air above my head and the SUV's engine roars as it takes off down the street.

I'm on my feet running, sprinting after it, and I catch a momentary glimpse of Addie's terrified face in the back window, her hand against the glass and her mouth open in an unheard scream, pleading with me to save her. The SUV speeds off leaving me stranded on the sidewalk. I turn and run back toward the office, thinking that I'll get the keys to my car and try to follow. I'm consumed with fear now, not thinking clearly. What are they going to do with my daughter? Where are they taking her? As I reach the wreckage that used to be my office, I see a woman lying on the sidewalk, blood pooling rapidly underneath her. She looks vaguely familiar. I roll her onto her back and gasp. It's Jessie, my wife. There is a gash across her throat and blood is spurting from the terrifying wound. How did she get here? I don't understand. She sees me and reaches her hand toward me.

"Save me, John! Save our daughter! Save us!"

Her hand falls limp to her side as the light is extinguished from her eyes and I scream out in grief.

"No! No! Don't leave me Jessie! Don't go!"

I start working on her, compressing her chest and screaming out, "Help! Someone! Call an ambulance! I'm sorry, Jessie! I'm sorry! Don't leave me like this!"

A dense fog rolls in and I hear the voice of Mortimer, my father-in-law, saying, "What sort of a husband are you? You couldn't save your wife and now you can't even protect your daughter!"

I open my eyes in the darkness of the lounge room to find that I am sobbing. Even though I now realize it was only a dream, the emotions that have risen to the surface overwhelm me. Tears stream down my face as I cry for the love that I lost. I am overwhelmed for several minutes, lost in grief and drowning in guilt. Deep down I know that Mort is right. It's my fault that Jessie is dead. I should have trained her in self-defense, and I shouldn't have let her go jogging on her own at night. And now I've placed my daughter in grave danger as well.

As the echoes of the dream fade and my tears finally dry up, I sit in the dark thinking through my options. Eventually I go to bed and sleep fitfully. I still don't have a clear plan, but one thing has changed. I am determined not to be a passive victim. I will do whatever it takes to protect my daughter, even if that means taking the fight to the bad guys.

14

____

I fall into a deep sleep eventually, and I wake to the sound of Quinn's bike in the parking lot below. My bedside clock reads 8:37 am. I roll out of bed still dressed in my clothes from last night. I wasn't going to be caught in my pajamas again if I was attacked. I grab the compact Glock 26 from the nightstand and stick it in my pocket, then I check the second drawer. My larger Glock 19 is still under my socks. What can I say? I'm a Glock man. I close the drawer and head downstairs and open up the office.

"Jeez! I hope you don't feel as bad as you look!" says Quinn as I greet her in the kitchen. "Because if you do, I need to call an ambulance."

"Thanks very much."

"You're welcome. The truth will set you free, dude."

She's mixing some sort of green concoction that looks like grass clippings.

"You're not seriously going to drink that are you?"

"What do you suggest I do with it? Squirt it up my ass?"

"You may as well, because that stuff looks like it's going to go straight through you."

I leave her to ingest her vile brew while I go back upstairs. I change into running gear and hit the streets, asking Quinn to look after the office for a while. An hour later, I've blown the cobwebs out and I'm feeling a lot better. As I shower, however, I notice that the wound on my side is red and swollen, and the bottom edge of the gash is oozing nasty-looking gunk. I hit it with some more antiseptic and put a fresh bandage over it, hoping that that will fix the problem. I need a strong coffee this morning, so I pay Costa a visit.

"Mr. John! There you are! I was worried you had gone somewhere else."

"Never. Your coffee's the best."

"Of course it is, my friend. What will you have?"

"Vienna espresso with whipped cream."

"Good choice! Good choice!"

A couple of minutes later, after assuring him that this morning's coffee is the best he's ever made, I'm back at my desk sipping my long black. I'm going to have to look up more coffee orders, because I'm starting to run out of variations.

Quinn is busy at her laptop and brings me up to date on her ongoing investigation into the Eskimo gang.

"I've scanned the CCTV footage near the home of our pal, Antonio Sanchez. At 6:15 pm yesterday, his car travels past the camera near his street, heading toward the industrial area. I follow it through three cameras and then it disappears in the same area as last time. At 3:10 this morning it retraces the route in reverse. Sanchez is obviously going home to bed."

"OK. Let's check again tomorrow morning and see if there is a definite nightly pattern to this."

"And then what?"

"I haven't exactly worked that bit out yet. Have you managed to find anything in the hospital records for Cory Wainwright?"

"Yes and no. I can confirm that his digital birth file in the birthing unit is blank, apart from his name. But then it gets very interesting."

She pauses and looks at me.

"Go on. I'm all ears."

"Data on hard drives is stored in individual bits consisting of either a one or a zero in a specific physical location on the drive. Erasing a bit of data doesn't immediately erase the one or zero, it simply removes the link to that bit. The data remains there until it is overwritten by further data storage which might utilize that same location."

I raised my hand in the air and she looks at me curiously.

"Yes?"

"Is this the interesting bit, or is it still coming?"

"OK, maybe I'll just cut to the chase."

"I'd really appreciate that, because I haven't got as long to live as you."

"I ran a sophisticated packet analyzing software across Cory's file and found that there was originally data there, but it's been deleted."

"Can it be retrieved?"

"If it had been deleted recently it might have been possible to retrieve it, depending on how many bits have been written over in the meantime by new data. However, since this file is twenty-nine years old, the chances are zero. But at least we know that the reason for the file being empty isn't simply because someone forgot to enter the data. Someone has deliberately deleted it."

I stand and start pacing around the room.

"OK. At this point we know two things. Firstly, at some point in the week between the birth of the first baby and Cory's appearance at the baby health clinic, one baby was switched for another. That seems pretty clear now. Secondly, someone has deleted the original data on the birth file, presumably to hide the discrepancy between the original baby and the new one."

"Yep. It sure looks that way," agrees Quinn.

I continue walking and thinking out loud.

"But there's a whole lot of things we don't know. Who erased the data? Someone on the hospital staff or a hacker from outside? What happened to the original baby? Where did the new baby come from? Who else knew about it? And why was the first baby swapped in the first place?"

I stop as a thought strikes me. I turn to Quinn.

"Cory's parents were clearly aware of the swap. The differences are too gross for them to be unaware. They definitely knew. More than that, I assume they were complicit. So, what would cause a mother to give up a baby she has carried for nine months, a baby she has given birth to, and swap it for a baby that isn't her own?"

"Maybe it was sick."

I nod. "That's what I'm thinking. Maybe it was very sick."

I sit back down at my laptop and do a quick google search: 'Life-threatening abnormalities among newborns." A whole range of diseases and abnormalities pops up. Too many to isolate a single likely scenario. I look at Quinn.

"I think we need to assume that 'Cory version one' was very sick. Can I get you to investigate what kind of newborn testing the hospital would have done back then? Particularly testing that was sent away for analysis. Then see if there are outside testing agencies or laboratories that might have retained their own records of those results."

"Roger, Obi-Wan Kenobi."

"And use the force if you have to," I add.

She laughs.

"While you're doing that, I have to go out for some very boring surveillance. I could be gone for quite a while. Do you want me to lock the front door?"

"No. I'll be fine. I'm your assistant, remember? I can handle any new clients who walk through the door. I can at least get their basic details and open a file for them."

"OK. But be nice to them. Try not to scare them off."

"I'm not that scary, dude."

"Yeah, well you're not exactly Mary Poppins either."

I grab my digital camera and telescopic lens from my bottom drawer and head out to the car. The subject, the man with the supposed back injury, lives in a rented property in Los Gatos. I arrive in his street to find his beat-up pickup truck in his driveway, so I assume he is home. Surveillance is always a hit and miss affair. He could easily have been out somewhere and I would have wasted a trip. I park down the street and settle in for a long wait. There is no view into his backyard so I can't hope for an easy photo of him doing anything strenuous there. Of course, his injury may be entirely genuine, which is why I budget for a maximum of five days of surveillance. Insurance companies generally won't pay for much more than that. While I'm waiting for something to happen, my mind drifts back to the Cory Wainwright case. I phone Quinn and give her another task: track down the contact details of any nurses or midwives who might have been on duty at the time of the birth. It's a long shot, but someone may remember something.

Two hours later I'm starving and kicking myself for not stocking my new car with nibbles. I'm just about to head to some local shops for food, when the subject walks out of his front door, wheeling a mountain bike. This looks promising. He wheels the bike to his truck then pauses, looking carefully up and down the street. Seeing no one, he effortlessly hoists the bike into the back of his truck – a maneuvre that would surely not be possible if he had a serious back injury. My telephoto lens captures the action perfectly.

He backs his truck out of the driveway and roars up the street, away from me. I follow at a discreet distant, already guessing where he is probably heading. I'm right. After a couple of blocks he turns onto Santa Cruz Highway and heads south. There is a lot of traffic on the highway, and I drop back, allowing a few cars to get between us. I can never work out why Hollywood always makes tailing another car so obvious. The people being followed must be complete idiots not to notice a car following them only twenty yards directly behind.

As expected, he turns off toward St. Joseph's Hill Preserve, where there are some fabulous walking and bike trails. I stay well back and when he turns onto Alma Bridge Road, I stop for almost a full minute, letting him get completely out of sight. Hoping I've timed it right, I start off again and drive fairly quickly for a few hundred yards before spotting his car parked exactly where I thought it would be.

I pull over, stop the car and quickly focus my camera on him through my front windscreen. He is standing beside his truck and takes a last long drag on his cigarette before flicking it into some nearby bushes. He reaches into the back of his truck and effortlessly lifts the bike out, then grabs a pump, bends down and attaches it to the valve on his front tire. He pumps both tires up in this way, bending right down to attach and detach the pump in both instances. I capture it all on camera and I now have enough evidence to satisfy my client and discredit the man's claim. But he saves the best till last. As he starts to ride down the trail, I get several shots of him executing an impressive jump over a large ridge of dirt and landing so heavily that even my back aches in sympathy.

Job done!

I celebrate by buying a double pastrami on rye and a mineral water at a nearby gas station and I sit in the car eating lunch at a nearby park. Bacteria never tasted so good. Because I've finished earlier than anticipated, I spontaneously decide to make a detour and visit St Aidan's Private Hospital on the way home. I may as well do a bit of preliminary investigation on the Cory Wainwright case while I'm nearby. The hospital isn't very far out of my way and as I drive into the hospital parking lot, I still haven't formed a clear plan of what I'm hoping to achieve. I guess I'm just curious.

I walk through the main entrance and follow the signs to the maternity wing. The double doors to the wing are closed but when I push one of them it opens, so I walk in and try to look as if I know where I'm going. Although the rest of the hospital seems tired and old, the maternity wing looks relatively new. I walk down a long, wide corridor with private rooms opening off it on either side. There is the sound of several babies crying and I see one woman shuffling very slowly down the corridor ahead of me, holding the handrail on the wall with one hand and holding her stomach with the other. If I was to guess, I'd say she's had a C-section and is only just getting back on her feet.

I notice that at several points along the corridor there are pamphlet racks, displaying promotional material for various community services for new mothers and their babies. I stop at one of the racks and scan the pamphlets: baby health clinics, playgroups, mothers support groups, antenatal depression support, home help services and more. My eye catches a strange inclusion; a pamphlet for an adoption agency. I lift one out and look more closely. 'Acorn Adoption Agency'. Its motto says, 'Let us care for your unwanted baby – because every child is precious'.

"Excuse me sir, visiting hours aren't until 4:00 pm. This is mothers' rest time. I'll have to ask you to leave."

I turn and see a matronly-looking nurse with a clipboard in her hand. Her mouth is smiling but her eyes are definitely not.

"I'm very sorry, I don't want to disturb anyone," I say.

I pull an ID out of my top pocket. I've had a card made up

which says 'P.I. John Targett' with a catchy logo that looks vaguely like a police shield but is just different enough to keep me out of legal trouble. I have the ID in a flip-open plastic pouch, almost identical to those used by police detectives. There is nothing illegal about it, but if I flash it quickly enough, some people might get confused and think I'm a police officer. Of course, this is an unfortunate misunderstanding over which I have no control.

I flash the ID quickly and say, "I'm PI John Targett, and I'm here on an investigation. Do you mind if I ask why you have brochures for an adoption agency in these display racks?"

She looks at me sternly as if debating whether to answer my question or have me thrown out. Finally, she gives in and says, "Not every woman who gives birth here is in a position to care for and raise a child. We think it's important that women know that they have choices. Sometimes both the woman and the baby will lead better lives if the baby is given up for adoption."

"I see. Is that option actively promoted?"

"Not overtly. But we do mention it to single mothers whom we feel are in high-risk groups."

"High risk for who? The baby or the mother?"

"Both. We want both mother and baby to have the best possible life."

"I see. What about babies who are born with serious abnormalities or diseases? Are there occasions when the mother of such a baby might give it up for adoption because she feels she won't be able to cope?"

"It has been known to happen."

"Do you keep a record of such adoptions?

"No that is strictly an arrangement between the parents and the agency."

She gives me a suspicious look and asks, "What police department did you say you were with?"

"That's all I needed, ma'am. Thank you for your time."

I turn and walk out of the ward, feeling as though she's drilling holes into my back with her eyes. She has obviously mistaken me for a police detective. I wonder how that happened?

15

———

I arrive back at the office to find the front door locked. I let myself in and start uploading today's photos to my laptop. After a few minutes, Quinn comes through the curtained partition from the back hallway.

"Sorry. I had to go to the bathroom. I thought I'd better lock the front door."

"It's a wonder you haven't been sitting on the toilet all day after drinking those grass clippings this morning."

"Very funny. By the way, I've been meaning to compliment you on this delightful green and orange striped material that you've got hanging in the doorway. Is there a particular reason you went with those colors?"

"The shop had run out of pink and purple stripes."

"What a shame."

"Have you made any progress with the Cory Wainwright case?"

"Sure have!" she enthuses. "It turns out that every newborn baby in the United States is automatically tested for a number of genetic abnormalities and diseases. A small blood sample is taken from every baby via a heel prick, usually on the day of its birth. In California, the sample is sent to CLNS, the California Laboratory for Neonatal Screening. They test each sample for thirty-four different genetic diseases. If the test is all negative, nothing further happens. If it is positive for a genetic disease, they inform the hospital and they also pass on the information to the national body – ASNS, the American Society for Neonatal Screening. ASNS keeps a detailed data base of all genetic diseases in newborn babies nationwide."

Quinn gives me a sly grin. "I managed to sneak into the data bases for both the California laboratory and the ASNS."

"Of course you did."

"Both data bases list all detected abnormalities according to date, and also list the baby's name and the hospital where the blood sample originated. On 16th September, two days after Cory's birth, his name shows up in both data bases as testing positive for two serious diseases; cystic fibrosis and phenylketonuria."

"I take it they're not good diseases to have?"

"No. Cystic fibrosis, or CF, is a disease where someone is basically perpetually drowning in their own mucus. It results in lung disease, digestive problems, poor weight gain, chronic infections, liver disease, diabetes and even heart failure. Phenylketonuria, or PKU, can be just as bad. Too much phenylalanine builds up in the body, causing seizures, delayed development, intellectual disability, behavioral problems, psychiatric disorders and a range of physical illnesses."

"And the original Cory had both those diseases?"

"Yep. He lost the genetic lottery twice."

"So, Mrs Wainwright would have known this, two days after giving birth, while she was still in the hospital?"

"Definitely. The hospital would have received the results electronically on the 16th and they would have informed Mrs Wainwright straight away, or at least the very next day."

I sit back in my chair and contemplate what I've just heard.

"I suppose to be completely thorough, we should check with Cory to confirm that he doesn't suffer from either of those two diseases."

"I already called him. He's as fit as a bull – in his own words."

"Nice work," I compliment her. "So now we know why the switch took place. The next step is to find out how. I think I might have a lead we can follow, but I suggest we start on that tomorrow. What about the staff? Is there any possibility that we can contact someone who was there when the baby was born?"

Quinn shakes her head. "It's going to be very difficult. There are no digital duty rosters in existence dating that far back. I managed to sneak into the HR data base, and I have a list of eight obstetricians and twelve midwives who were registered as working in the hospital in that year. I guess we could call them all and ask if they remember the birth."

"Mm ... it sounds like a long shot. Let's think about it overnight. I think we've accomplished enough for one day. We should give ourselves the rest of the afternoon off."

Perfectly on cue, Addie walks through the door and dumps her school bag on the floor.

"Hi guys! How's the detective business going?"

I look at my watch and see that it's 4:15.

"How was the hot date with your gym teacher?" I counter.

She shakes her head and rolls her eyes at me. It's starting to be a standard response.

Addie and Quinn end up watching YouTube clips on Quinn's laptop while I quickly bash out a final report on 'mountain bike man' for the insurance company. I hear the girls chatting happily in the background, but once again they seem to be conversing in a foreign language. They discuss artists that I've never heard of, saying that someone is 'extra', an album is 'straight fire', and someone else is too 'flex'. Then I hear Quinn say, "I don't care what they say. Kanye's dope and the new album is lit."

At last I know who they are talking about and I feel I have something worthwhile to contribute to the conversation.

"I wouldn't necessarily describe Kanye West as particularly stupid. He must have some business smarts to be doing so well."

The two girls look up from their screen and stare at me. Addie has a pained expression on her face. Quinn turns to her and says, "Go easy on him. At least he's trying." Addie just shakes her head and gives me a sad look, then both girls go back to watching the next video. I have no idea what I've just said.

I finish my report and fire off an email to the insurance company, attaching photos along with my invoice for the job. Then I head upstairs to the bathroom where I've left the medical kit. I've been in increasing pain all afternoon and it's starting to become unbearable. I take my shirt off and the sight that greets me isn't good. My whole left side is angry, red and swollen. I take the bandage off. The wound is starting to look nasty. It's inflamed and swollen and the sutures are stretched tight across the weeping cut. I reapply antiseptic cream and put a fresh bandage on, but I have a feeling that I'm fighting a losing battle. I need professional help.

Half an hour later I drop Addie off at Karl and Billie's, with Quinn following on her bike. I thank them again for their help and they invite me to stay for dinner but I excuse myself, saying that I've got some work to do.

It's 5:45 pm by the time I walk into O'Connor Hospital Emergency Department. I'm in luck. There are only two prospective patients in the waiting room: a guy supporting his right arm gingerly, accompanied by his girlfriend; and a mother with a baby. I'm hoping that I may not have to wait too long before being seen. It takes a whole hour before the guy with the sore arm gets called in, and another fifty minutes before the mother and baby get seen to. In the meantime, four more people have taken chairs in the waiting room, including an elderly man who smells like he hasn't had a shower in a year. I hate hospital emergency departments.

It's 8:30 by the time I'm finally called into the consulting rooms. I'm shown to a cubicle where a pleasant male nurse removes the dressing and gives the wound an initial clean before going to fetch a doctor. Another fifteen minutes pass before a doctor finally arrives.

My opinion of O'Connor Hospital dramatically improves the moment she walks through the curtain. Dr. Claire Peters is stunning. She has a classic kind of beauty; fine features, porcelain skin and just a light smattering of freckles across the bridge of her dainty nose, which only enhances her attractiveness, giving her that wholesome 'girl-next-door' look. Her vivid green eyes are offset by her long dark hair, which is currently tied back in a neat ponytail.

"Hi. I'm Claire. What have you done to yourself?"

She has a refined English accent and a soft, gentle voice. I think I'm in love.

"Cut myself a couple of days ago on some broken glass."

She looks carefully at the wound.

"Where did you get the sutures done?"

"Um. I did them myself, at home."

She shakes her head and 'tut tuts' at me. "That was a bit silly. Looks like you've got a nasty infection there now."

She snaps some gloves on and starts gently pressing on me, initially in a wide circle around the wound, but then on the wound itself. I grit my teeth and can't help groaning.

"Did you flush the wound and disinfect it before suturing?"

"I dabbed disinfectant on it. I wouldn't exactly say I flushed it."

"Well, I'd say that's your problem. You've probably got some grit trapped in there. I'm sorry to do this to you, but I'm going to have to open the wound up again and give it a thorough clean."

"Sure. As long as you give me a local anesthetic. I don't think I could go through the suturing a second time without numbing it."

"You sutured without anesthetic?"

"Yeah. Never again."

She just shakes her head in disbelief and starts to work. She injects anesthetic quite deeply all around the wound, which almost sends me through the roof. The anesthetic takes affect almost immediately, however, and she gets to work, snipping, slicing and sluicing. After a few minutes she reaches into the wound with some tweezers and extracts a small chunk of glass and another piece of dark-colored grit.

"There's your problem," she says, proudly displaying the offending items in a silver tray. She finishes cleaning and disinfecting the wound, then sutures it closed, quickly and expertly.

"You'll have to teach me how to do that," I say.

"I'll do no such thing, thank you very much!" she says in mock indignation. "No more self-doctoring for you. And that's an order!"

"Yes, ma'am," I say, smiling.

She smiles back at me and I feel my whole world tilt into a new kind of alignment.

She straightens up and admires her handiwork, then she has a closer look at my swollen red side.

"That's fixed the wound up nicely," she says, "but unfortunately the infection has already spread to the surrounding area. I'll be giving you a prescription for oral antibiotics to take for the next ten days, but to be safe, I think I should give you a rapid infusion of intravenous antibiotics to get on top of the infection."

"You mean a drip?"

"Just for an hour. You don't have to be anywhere urgently do you?"

"Not at all. I'll be very happy staying here for as long as you like," I say, looking directly at her.

She blushes slightly and turns away, busying herself as she prepares her equipment. The cannula is inserted and a drip attached, and for the next forty-five minutes I sit upright in the bed doing nothing. Claire comes in several times to check on the flow of the drip, and each time she does, my heart rate seems to increase. We banter lightly and I can't help feeling that there is a vibe between us.

I've never been more reluctant to leave an emergency department in my life, but eventually I have to. Claire walks me to the door leading back into the reception area and gives me strict instructions to take the full course of antibiotics. As she opens the door for me, I say, somewhat foolishly, "I'll have to think of some way of injuring myself, so I can come back and see you again."

"I'd prefer that you didn't."

I must look disappointed, because she quickly clarifies her meaning.

"Injure yourself, I mean. Not the ... second bit."

I walk out into the night air feeling a mixture of hope and confusion. It's the first time I've experienced a quickening of interest toward a woman since Jessie died. Maybe I'm not completely broken inside after all. Perhaps I should think about asking Claire out? But then I think of Addie and my complicated life with my strange work hours, and suddenly it just seems too hard to try and fit another person into all of that. I'd almost asked for Claire's phone number a moment ago, but I chickened out at the last moment. Now I'm glad that I didn't ask.

As I walk back to my car, I chide myself for my foolishness. It's just Addie and me from now on, and I'm content with that.

16

I wake just before six the next morning and take a second antibiotic capsule, having taken the first one last night after getting the prescription filled at an all-night pharmacy. I slept fitfully, refusing to take the painkillers that the doctor had given me on the way out, but the wound is definitely feeling a lot better this morning.

Five minutes after getting out of bed, I'm running, pounding the pavement, the chill morning air shocking me fully awake like a dose of smelling salts. I only go for a short run, however, because I have something else in mind this morning. When I get back, I set up my martial arts training tower which has been folded in a corner of the storeroom. I unfold the various arms of the six-foot tower. Each arm has multiple pads attached at different heights and angles. I haven't practiced for days and I'm looking forward to the session, but I will need to be careful not to bust open my stitches.

I start with some basic warm up maneuvres and quickly click into a familiar groove. After a while, I start increasing the pace, enjoying the burn that comes to my muscles and feeling the flow of energy as I execute familiar routines. I introduce more complex moves, requiring my full concentration now. Spin, kick, pivot, punch, twist, strike. Repeat. My balance is a little out after a few days off, but it soon comes back and I am able to gradually increase my intensity to full power. The impacts on the pads now sound like gunshots in the confines of the storeroom, and I am reveling in the feeling of explosive power.

I keep it up for a solid thirty minutes and eventually finish with a warm-down routine that involves a series of smooth, slower movements. Finally, I hold myself in a plank position on the floor while I count off five minutes on my watch. My side is killing me by now, but I can see through the clear plastic tape that covers the wound that the sutures are all still intact.

By the time Quinn arrives I'm back at my desk, showered and changed, sipping a Beanstalk coffee and checking emails.

"Any luck with Angry Birds?" she asks as she walks to her desk with her morning cup of soggy grass clippings.

"No, I've given up."

"Good idea. Stick to bingo at the local seniors' club."

She fires up her laptop and asks, "What do you want me to start on this morning, boss?"

I explain to her about my visit to St Aidan's Hospital yesterday, and I show her the adoption agency brochure that I found there.

"So you think the adoption agency could be involved in the baby switch?" she asks.

"I know it's a long shot, but it's the best place to start looking. After all, we've somehow got to explain how one baby could disappear and another one appear in its place. The Wainwrights couldn't have done that by themselves; they must have been resourced by some kind of outside agency."

"It could all be perfectly legal, couldn't it?" Quinn asks.

"There's certainly nothing illegal about giving your baby up for adoption. Nor is there anything illegal about adopting a new baby. But there are two factors that have the smell of corruption about them: the duplicity and the timing. The new baby was given a false name; the name of another baby. And in terms of timing there's a major problem as well. The swap took place within a few short days; between giving birth on the 14th and visiting the baby health clinic on the 21st. Also, for the switch to go unnoticed as it apparently did, it had to be before anyone in the outside world saw the first baby, as the two babies look totally different."

"That also means the switch couldn't have happened while the mother was still in hospital," adds Quinn, "otherwise the nurses would have noticed the difference."

"Good point. Which means the switch could really only have taken place after leaving the hospital and before arriving home, where they would surely be receiving visitors and family. In fact, the only way this could have worked was for no family to have visited the new baby and mother while they were in the hospital."

Quinn nods her head. "The more you think about it, the harder it seems that anyone could have pulled this off at all."

"Plus, there's one other issue of timing that's extremely problematic," I continue. "If we suppose that the Wainwrights drove straight from the hospital to an adoption agency, offloaded one baby and were given another, we have to consider how unlikely even that scenario is. To adopt a baby takes many months of bureaucratic paperwork. You simply can't adopt a baby in a few days. Not legally."

"So, what do you want me to do?"

"Two things. Firstly, see if you can find out when Helen Wainwright and her baby were discharged. That will help us clarify the timing. Secondly, do some investigating of Acorn Adoption Agency. See if you can find any adoption records of babies either being given up for adoption or babies being adopted out, for the week in question."

"What about death certificates?" she asks. "Perhaps the first baby died."

"There can't be a death certificate, because the person we know as Cory still bears the first baby's name."

"Right. Of course. That makes sense. What about our friendly Eskimo gang? Do you want me to keep tracking the late-night car movements for Antonio Sanchez?"

"No. Don't worry about that for the moment. I'm hoping that will just fade away now. I think they've paid us their one and only visit. Let's focus on the Cory Wainwright case."

Quinn wanders into the kitchen to fix a bowl of muesli. While she's gone, I phone a local sign writer and he agrees to come out tomorrow morning and paint a new business sign on the front window. I make two more phone calls and when Quinn gets back to her desk, I tell her I'm heading out.

Cory's sister, Caroline, has agreed to meet with me this morning. Cory has already cued her up and told her what I'm investigating. She's a work-from-home mom who runs an online business selling home-made jewelry, and the living room where we eventually sit to talk is bursting with bottles of glass beads and containers of shiny doodads.

"Cory's told you what he's asking me to investigate?" I ask, gently.

"Yes. We discovered the photograph and the birth record together. I still can't quite believe it."

"It must be quite a shock."

"It certainly is. I've lived all my life believing that Cory was my natural brother, and now it seems he isn't at all. I can't even imagine how he must be feeling."

"I know you were young when he was born. Do you have any memory at all of his birth?"

"A little. I was seven. I later found out that my parents had trouble conceiving again after me. That's why there's such a gap between Cory and me."

"What can you remember? Did you see your baby brother in hospital?"

"No. I remember Dad saying that no one was allowed to visit Mom in hospital, in case we gave germs to the new baby. The first time I saw Cory was when Dad and Mom drove up the driveway and lifted the baby pod out of the back seat. Grandma was minding me at the time."

"Looking back now, can you think of anything your parents said or did that might give an indication that Cory wasn't your natural brother?"

"No. Nothing whatsoever."

"You said you were home when they arrived back from hospital. You were school-aged. So it must have either been after school hours or on the weekend. Can you remember which it was?"

"Definitely. It was a Sunday. I know for sure, because Grandma took me to mass that morning and, after the service, we lit a candle for my new baby brother. I was still in my Sunday clothes when they came home."

"Anything else of significance about that day? Anything unusual?"

"No. Sorry. I can't think of anything else."

I can't think of anything else to ask either, so I thank her and leave.

Fifteen minutes later I pull up into the parking lot of the Acorn Adoption Agency. This place seriously reeks of money! It is a magnificent two-level building surrounded by about an acre of beautifully manicured gardens. I park in the visitors' parking lot and walk through the main entrance and find myself in a plush, expansive lobby with enough potted plants to warrant a full-time gardener. There is soft music playing through a hidden sound system, and the furniture and décor look like they could be featured in a home decorating magazine. I approach the curved timber reception desk and I'm greeted by a receptionist who could easily be a fashion model.

"Good morning, sir, how may I help you?" she says, showing me her artificially whitened teeth.

"Hi. My wife and I are considering adoption and I was just passing by and thought I would drop in to get some preliminary information."

"Certainly sir. Normally you would need to make an appointment, but if you'd like to take a seat I can check with our team of consultants and see if someone is available."

"No need for that at this stage," I assure her. "My wife would like to be here with me for that interview. I just wanted to see if you had any brochures that I could take home."

"Certainly, sir." She swivels her chair and grabs several brochures from a rack behind her. She hands them to me one at a time, giving a brief explanation of each one as she does so. There are three brochures: 'Adoption Laws of California', 'Finding the Right Child for You' and 'Adoption: What to Expect'.

Once she's finished her spiel I ask, "Can you tell me roughly how long the whole process might take?"

"That very much depends on the sort of child you're interested in adopting. Children from minority groups are more readily available, as are older children. In those cases, the whole adoption process might only take a few months. The demand for Caucasian, first-world children is, of course, much greater, and the process usually takes considerably longer. Generally speaking, the younger the child, the longer the wait. Finding and matching you to a newborn baby can take several years."

"I see. And can you give me a rough estimate of the cost involved?"

"Once again, sir, that depends on the child and the country of origin. There are many factors to be considered. You could be looking at somewhere between twenty and fifty thousand dollars."

"OK. Well, thank you. You've been very helpful. I'll talk it over with my wife and we'll be back in contact if we want to take it further."

I head back to the car with a new line of enquiry to pursue.

17

The sign writer has finished and there's an invoice from him sitting on my desk when I get back. Quinn is still sitting at her desk, working on her laptop. She's got a Beanstalk takeout cup beside her.

"Any walk-ins while I was gone?" I ask.

"Nope.

"Did you have any success with the hospital discharge date?"

"17th September."

"Excellent!" I start to look up a calendar for that year, but Quinn is one step ahead of me.

"That was a Thursday. She was admitted on the Sunday and gave birth early Monday morning."

"Well that's very interesting," I say. "Because Cory's sister says that her mom and the new baby definitely came home on a Sunday. So what were they doing from Thursday to Sunday?"

"Doing a baby swap, obviously."

"Yes. But where? And how is that even possible in such a short space of time? I just paid the Acorn Adoption Agency a brief visit and got a basic idea of average adoption timeframes.

We're talking months for older children and years for babies. You just can't walk in off the street and pick up a baby in a few days."

"Not legally," adds Quinn.

"I think you're right. That's where all this is heading. Because what happened in Cory's case was not baby adoption; it was baby substitution. And it happened in the space of a few days. Did you manage to get into Acorn's files? Are there any adoption records for the week in question?"

"No. There's nothing on their servers dating from that long ago."

"I guess I half expected that. And even if there were records dating back that far, I'm starting to think that this transaction isn't going to be on their legitimate books. Which brings me to the issue of money. A normal adoption costs anywhere up to fifty grand. I'm guessing the Wainwrights ended up paying much more than that for their baby swap. Perhaps we could try and trace the money. Would there be digital bank records going back nearly 30 years?"

"Possibly, but they wouldn't be accessible online. They would be kept on a separate server at the bank. And even if it were possible to hack into it, I'm not prepared to do that. Hacking a bank is a serious felony."

"Of course. And I wouldn't ask you to do that. But there might be a way around it. I'll phone Cory. He might be able to ask for his parents' bank records, especially if he's executor to their will."

"Cool. By the way, while you were out, I had some spare time, so I checked up on our pal, Antonio Sanchez. He did pretty much the same thing again last night. Drove his car to that industrial area to the north of Santa Clara a little after six, and stayed there until nearly four in the morning, then drove home again."

"OK. Good information. There's definitely a pattern there,

but I'm inclined to drop the whole thing now. Let sleeping dogs lie."

It's lunchtime and I suggest that we take a break.

"What do you want me to do this afternoon?"

"Do you know anything about security cameras?" I ask.

"Yeah. I was involved in sourcing some for the software company I worked for. What are you looking for?"

"I'm thinking of getting a couple of discreet cameras installed; one in the entrance foyer and one here in the office."

"No problem. I'll look into it."

She leaves soon after on her bike, and I head upstairs to fix myself a sandwich.

After lunch, I phone Cory and bring him up to date on our progress so far. I ask if he can try and get hold of his parents' bank records from the year of his birth and he says he'll see what he can do. My only other active case now is the potentially cheating partner. As it's Thursday today, which is the night when the man supposedly goes bowling, I call the young woman, Kelly, and ask if her partner, Jason, is planning to go bowling tonight. She tells me that he is, and says he usually leaves home about eight. I tell her I'll probably do some surveillance tonight and let her know if I find anything suspicious.

After that, it's a quiet afternoon so I take the opportunity to finish a book review I've been working on for the New York Times. The book, 'A Long Look Over the Back Fence', was promoted as a break-through work of literature by a rising new author, but I found it dull and cumbersome. I finish my review and send it off to the editor. It's a well-written review of a disappointing book, and I will be paid well for it.

After that is done, I place an advertisement in the local paper for my investigative services. I don't often advertise, as most of my work comes from insurance companies with whom I have an ongoing relationship, but when business is slow, an ad in the newspaper will often pull in one or two new domestic clients.

Because I'll be out on surveillance tonight, I want Addie and Quinn to stay one more night with Karl and Billie, just to be on the safe side. We're planning a takeout pizza dinner here first, before I drop Addie off. By 5:30, all three of us are upstairs, looking at the takeout pizza menu, trying to decide what to order.

"Do they have a Fruit Loop pizza?" I ask. "That way you could have leftovers for breakfast tomorrow as well."

"Very funny, Dad."

We end up ordering three; a vegetarian for Quinn, ham and pineapple for Addie and seafood for me. When they arrive, we sit around the dining table, something Addie and I rarely do, as we tend to eat at the kitchen bench.

"Gross! That looks disgusting!" exclaims Addie as I take a bite of my marinara pizza. "Are those actual octopus tentacles?"

"Baby octopus," I say as I momentarily dangle a particularly large tentacle in front of her and then pop it into my mouth. I chew it in an exaggerated fashion and swallow, then comment, "Right about now, there's a mommy and daddy octopus saying, 'I wonder where Junior is? He's very late getting home from school'."

"Dad! That's so grody!"

"She means, 'disgusting'," says Quinn, helpfully.

"Yes. I gathered that." I point at Addie's pizza. "You do realize, don't you, that the yellow stuff is actually fruit? As in, something from a plant that's grown out of the ground."

"It's OK," she replies, speaking with a mouthful. "It's been sanitized in a hot oven."

"Ah, yes. And all those nasty vitamins have been destroyed as well. We don't want your metabolism getting confused by having to deal with unfamiliar nutrients, do we?"

Quinn looks at Addie and says, "He's good. I rate him for sarcasm."

"You don't have to live with him," replies Addie. "Besides, I've heard all his material before. It wears a bit thin after a while."

I drop Addie off a little after seven, with Quinn following on her bike. I've invited Karl to come bowling with me, as I would look a bit conspicuous hanging around a bowling alley by myself. I've told him about the surveillance that I need to do and he's happy to come along to act as cover for me. Kelly, the woman I'm doing the investigation for, has previously told me the name of the bowling alley that Jason goes to, and says that he has a standing reservation for 8:00 pm. Just to be sure, I phoned the alley this afternoon to 'confirm' the reservation in Jason's name, which they did.

At about 7:15, Karl and I say goodbye and head out the door. As we walk down the path toward my car, Karl high fives me and says, "Target and Destroy are back in business, dude!"

Karl and I had been the two most popular instructors on the Joint Forces Training Base, and the term, 'Target and Destroy' had been applied to us by the trainees. It was a play on our last names, as Karl's surname is Destrier, a vestige of his distant French ancestry. My surname, with a double 'T' is also apparently French in origin, but I haven't bothered to trace it back to any specific French ancestors.

We take my car and ten minutes later we are parked a hundred yards from Kelly and Jason's house. Their only vehicle, a beat-up station wagon, is still sitting in the driveway. We sit there talking, relaxed in our friendship, reminiscing about life on the base. Karl reminds me of my martial arts duel with Colonel Squires, the base's second in command, soon after I arrived. He had a reputation on base for his exceptional close combat skills and he challenged me to a bout. Squires was a bit of a bastard and probably thought he'd flog me, as he had only recently won the ICCC, the Inter-services Close Combat Championship. A lot of betting took place in the lead up to our bout and I was pretty nervous. The event was held on a Saturday night and a large crowd had turned up to watch.

The bout was the first to ten throws and I started off badly. He sold me a dummy and threw me fairly quickly. That's when I got angry. I threw him ten times in a row after that and won the bout easily. I don't think he ever forgave me.

"I don't think there'll be anything quite as exciting happening tonight," I warn Karl, after he finishes reminiscing.

But I was wrong.

18

We pull into the parking lot of 'Texas Ten Pin' at five minutes to eight. We've tailed Jason all the way here and he hasn't diverted. The place is the tackiest bowling alley I think I've ever seen. The outside of the building is festooned with pictures of cowboys and cowgirls lit up with flashing colored lights. The cowboy theme continues inside, in just as tasteless a fashion. Karl and I hurry inside before Jason, and take up position at the bar, which is decorated like a wild west saloon. We watch as Jason walks in and is met by his mate. They look like a pigeon pair. Both are about six foot and at least 210 pounds and look like they do some heavy lifting in a gym. Their sleeveless shirts reveal impressive arms that are covered in tattoos. Jason has a shaved head and his mate has a mullet.

"I'm thinking roids," says Karl.

"Wouldn't be surprised," I agree.

We wait until they are allocated a lane and have chosen balls from the racks, then we go to the counter and hire a lane for ourselves. I figure we may as well have some fun while we're here. We end up two lanes away from them, with no one in the lane between. I'd prefer to be a little bit further away, but now that we're here I decide that as long as we keep a low profile it should be OK. We play two straight games, keeping pace with the 'roid boys', as Karl is now calling them. Karl is a better bowler than me, mainly because I never do it, and he and Billie are regulars. I'm just starting to think we're wasting our time when two young women in high heels, extremely short skirts and skin-tight tops walk through the front doors and waltz straight over to the boys. The brunette sits next to mullet head and gives him a long, lingering kiss, while blondie plonks herself down on Jason's lap and does likewise.

By then I've got my micro camera palmed in my hand and I manage to get a couple of shots of the action. They don't start another game, but just sit there making out and fondling. After a few minutes, mullet head and the brunette enter the disabled toilet together and lock the door. They're gone for about ten minutes. Then it's Jason and blondie's turn. I've seen enough. Karl and I go to the counter and pay up. I don't want to leave yet, however. I'm thinking we may as well hang around and finish the surveillance by tailing Jason when he leaves here, just in case there's more naughty action to report. We go to the bar and order drinks, a beer and a soda water, and sit drinking them while keeping an eye on the group.

The girls leave soon after Jason's session in the toilet, waving a saucy 'ta taa' as they walk back out the front doors. Jason and mullet head hang around for a few more minutes, changing shoes and returning balls, before leaving as well. I give them thirty seconds before we head out the door after them, with Karl still holding his half-finished stubby of Budweiser.

And that's when the fun starts.

We walk down the steps into the semi-dark parking lot and can't see the boys anywhere.

"Hey, dickheads! Are you looking for us?"

We turn around and see them step out of the shadows, from around the corner of the building.

"What are you? A couple of perverts? Can't get any chicks yourself, so you come down here to get your rocks off perving at other guys' girls?"

Damn! They'd obviously noticed us looking their way in the bowling alley. I'm surprised, because I'd been extremely careful, barely glancing at them. Perhaps Karl had been less subtle.

"I'm sorry," I say. "You're mistaken. We weren't looking at anyone. We just came here to bowl."

"Oooh! I'm Sorry! You're mistaken!" Jason says, mimicking my cultured accent. "What are you? A faggot?"

By now we are faced off. Karl is slightly behind me to my left. Jason is directly in front of me and mullet head is slightly behind him, to his left and my right.

"Look, we don't want any trouble. We certainly weren't looking at your girls."

"Bullshit! Your buddy was practically drooling!"

Jason steps forward and shoves me in the chest. He's got two inches and at least thirty pounds advantage over me, but I see it coming and brace myself with my left leg behind me and I don't budge. Jason is surprised, expecting me to be pushed backward. His eyes narrow and there's a steroid-fueled rage in his eyes that won't be denied. I am convinced now that I will have to fight him. There is no way we can walk unscathed to our car now, and even if we could, I don't want him to ID my vehicle. I decide to give him a last chance to disengage and go home.

"In that case we humbly apologize if we've offended you. Let's just call it quits and all go home."

"The only place you're going tonight is the hospital, you wanker!" he says, pushing me again.

But it's not enough for me to engage. We're probably in range of CCTV cameras. I need my next actions to be clearly in self-defense. I need him to take a swing at me and preferably, make contact.

"Need a hand, dude?" says Karl, calmly.

"No. I got this."

"Don't hurt them too much."

I look Jason in the eye and calmly say, "Are you going to stand there all night talking, or are you going to actually do something, you fat, ugly hillbilly."

Jason's eyes bulge and he does exactly what I expect him to do. He swings at me with a wild roundhouse punch. I've already noted earlier that he is right-handed, and as he's been talking, I've carefully estimated his reach. He has long arms, but he's also muscle-bound, so his reach will be slightly inhibited by over-developed biceps. His swing is slightly slower than I anticipated too, so I have to make a last-second adjustment for that as well. My head is already moving back and down to my right, and I allow him to hit me a glancing blow to my forehead. I continue to duck lower for a fraction of a second until I'm almost crouching and then I activate my quads and drive straight in toward him. I had been planning on a strike to his solar plexus but at the last moment I change my mind. He is taller than me and he is standing with his legs straddled wide apart. I can't resist the opening; his testicles are practically calling to me. I drive in and up with a vicious right-handed uppercut to his nuts. I put every ounce of strength into the blow and I don't miss.

It's enough to take him out of the fight for the next five minutes, but I'm now in an ideal position to finish him off and opportunities like that shouldn't be wasted. I always told my trainees to err on the side of aggression rather than caution, as you only get one chance at survival in a critical encounter. Jason's head is now moving downward as he doubles over in agony, so I continue to drive upward and smash my forehead into the bridge of his nose. There is a satisfying crunch and his body goes slack as he loses consciousness.

The whole maneuvre takes about a second, and mullet head is only just starting to react. I'm prepared to let him go if he decides to turn and run, but there's clearly not a lot of gray matter between his ears because he seems to fancy his chances. As Jason falls to the ground with a thud, his pal comes rushing in and swings a right then a left. I lean back out of reach of the right, which is a wild hook, and then see the left coming. He's also a right-hander and his left is cumbersome and slow. I step inside it and pivot clock-wise, grabbing his arm as it goes past my head, and pulling it down sharply while I dig my back and left hip into his stomach. It's a decent throw, and he lands on his back.

"Stay down! Don't get up!" I yell at him aggressively, pointing my finger at him as if he's a disobedient dog. But mullet head still fancies his chances, as I haven't yet landed a blow on him.

"I'm gonna kill you!" he yells, adding a colorful but completely unnecessary reference to the female anatomy. He rolls over and starts to get up, which leaves me with no choice.

Kicking someone in the head is incredibly dangerous and should not be attempted unless you really know what you are doing or you mean to kill them. The kill shot is the temple. A solid blow to that region of the head will immediately render someone unconscious. A more severe blow to that region can rupture several major blood vessels not far below the surface causing massive bleeding to the brain. I don't want to go near that area, but as mullet head is conveniently on his hands and knees right now, I am actually spoilt for other choices.

The two best options are a round house kick to the side of the jaw and forehead or a front kick, coming up under his jaw. Both will render him momentarily unconscious if I judge them properly, but the front kick will probably also result in breaking several teeth, whereas the roundhouse might only break his jaw. I decide to take pity on his teeth. I hope he appreciates my kindness later. The roundhouse connects perfectly and he flops over onto his side, like a good little doggy rolling over for his master.

The whole engagement has lasted less than thirty seconds, and I haven't raised a sweat.

"Fat, ugly hillbilly?" says Karl, as he slowly walks over, taking a sip out of his half-finished Budweiser. "That's the best you could come up with?"

"I was under pressure."

Karl just shakes his head. "You've really gotta work on your trash talk, dude. That was lame."

19

___

After placing both sleeping hillbillies in the recovery position and checking that they aren't in any danger, I drive Karl home. He thanks me and says it's the best night out he's had for ages. I say goodbye and drive a couple of blocks before stopping again. I phone Kelly, Jason's partner, and offer my apology, saying that I wasn't able to get to the bowling alley tonight after all. I tell her I'll try and go next week and I'll let her know if I discover anything.

You can call me a chicken if you like, but I don't want Jason to work out that the person who beat him up was probably the investigator that his wife hired to check up on him. Without a doubt, if I give Kelly my findings tonight or in the next few days and she confronts her partner with the evidence, even someone as stupid as Jason would make the connection. I've already put myself in the crosshairs with one lot of bad guys; I don't want to be constantly looking over my shoulder watching for a couple of angry meatheads at the same time.

The call to Kelly doesn't take long. As I finish and reach over to place my phone on the passenger seat, I feel a wet patch on my left side. I lift up my shirt to inspect the damage. Damn! I must have split open a couple of sutures when I threw the second guy. I check the time. It's just after eleven. I decide to swing by the hospital and check out the emergency ward. If it's busy, I'll go home and try to patch it up myself, although I will have to buy more surgical silk if I'm going to do that. Do all-night pharmacies sell that kind of stuff? I'm not sure. Perhaps I can ask at the hospital.

I walk into the emergency ward fifteen minutes later and utter an exasperated sigh. There are at least six people waiting. There's no way I'm going to sit here waiting all night. But somehow, I need to try and get some more silk. I walk to the reception desk and ask if they know where I might get some suture silk or if I could somehow buy some from the ED. The receptionist tries to fob me off but I'm insistent enough for her to eventually send me along to the next window, where the triage nurse is stationed. The nurse is banging away on her computer keyboard and so I wait at the window hoping to catch her eye. She eventually works out that I'm not going away and so she slides her window open and asks if she can help me. The English language is a fascinating thing. It's possible to say one thing and mean the exact opposite.

"Can I help you?" she asks, with a tone in her voice that actually means, 'Go away; can't you see I'm busy?'

I am in the middle of telling her that I just need to get some suture silk to sew up a wound that has opened again, when Dr Claire Peters walks past in the background. She glances my way and stops in her tracks, then walks over to the window.

"What are you doing here again?"

I start to explain and she interrupts, saying, "Come in, quickly, and I'll sort you out."

She leads me to a cubicle and tells me to take off my shirt and lie down. As she examines the wound, she says, "So last night, when you told me that you'd have to think up an excuse to come back and see me, you really weren't joking."

"Actually, I was joking, but now that I'm here, I'm not sorry that it's worked out this way."

She smiles at me and I feel a surge of ... I don't know ... something ... something good.

"So, how did you manage to ruin my perfectly good sutures?"

"I tripped over a hillbilly."

She raises her eyebrows at me, unsure what to make of that comment.

I watch her as she works. She has her dark hair tied back in a ponytail again, and she wears no makeup that I can see, but she is still as lovely as I remember. I notice that she does a cute little thing with her lips as she concentrates, and I start to fantasize about kissing her. I shake my head to try to snap myself out of it, and she seems to notice.

"Everything all right?" she asks.

"Yeah. Sorry. Daydreaming. Thinking of something that's clearly impossible."

"Sometimes, what initially looks impossible, isn't impossible at all."

She flicks me a meaningful look. Or at least I think that's what it is. But I'm no good at this stuff. Maybe she's just trying to work out how to get rid of me. Maybe she thinks I'm a stalker and she's considering calling security.

Changing the subject, I ask if she's often on night shift.

"Not really. I take my turn, like everyone else. I've got a couple of days off coming up, and after that I'll be back on a more reasonable shift."

There's a voice inside my head now, saying, *Ask her out! Ask her out!* But something's holding me back. Do I feel like I'm being unfaithful? Or am I just plain scared? I don't know.

She finishes tidying up. She had to give me a quick shot of anesthetic, then snip two sutures, pull them free and redo them in a slightly different spot, because the previous ones had torn through the flesh. After putting a new bandage on, she tells me that I'm free to go.

"Is there some paperwork I should have filled out?"

She smiles at me and says, "I won't tell if you don't."

It's a killer smile. It's her secret weapon. She could slay giants with that smile. She could bring wars to a halt and bring about world peace. She walks me to the door again and says, "Next time, if you want to see me, try to take a more conventional approach."

The door closes and she's gone, and I'm standing like a dummy in the waiting room, trying to figure out what she meant. *Next time?* Was that just a throw-away line, a joke at my expense, or is she saying she's interested in seeing me again? I haven't got a clue. I wish Addie was here to help me interpret.

I drive home and let myself into the apartment. It feels very empty without Addie. And then I realize something. Even when Addie is here, it still feels empty. The problem, of course, isn't the apartment. It's me. I'm lonely. I miss sharing my life with someone. I miss loving someone and being loved in return.

As I lie in bed a short time later, I reach an important decision. I'm going to ask Claire Peters out. The worst that can happen is that she says 'no'. Maybe I'm reading the signs incorrectly, but I won't know unless I take a chance. As Karl says, it's time to get back in the saddle. I just hope it doesn't hurt too much if I fall off.

20

I t's Friday and the day starts with a familiar pattern. Run, shower, breakfast, coffee. Quinn is in by 8:30 and as she drinks her slimy green concoction, we discuss living arrangements.

"I think it's safe to move back here, don't you?" she asks.

"Yes. I think so. The gang have made their point and it seems like it's over."

"Good. As much as I like your friends, it'll be nice to have my own space again."

"You'll be here on your own tonight, though," I say. "At least for a while. Addie's got another sleepover and I'm going over to Karl and Billie's. I'm taking them out for a nice meal to thank them for helping us this week."

"Cool. But don't sweat about me. I'm going out with some friends tonight anyway, to see a band. I might not even make it back here."

"That's salty," I say.

Quinn almost chokes on her green sludge and ends up spraying some across her desk, she's laughing so much. Once she returns from the brink of asphyxiation, she suggests that I stick to using words whose meanings I actually understand. Clearly, I need to do more research.

She then gives me a brief summary of the various security camera options that she discovered in her research yesterday. She shows me a few brochures and I decide on a very reasonably priced system with two tiny movement-activated cameras linked to a hard drive. The store that sells them is only two blocks away. I phone them and they advise me that as I'm nearby, they can do the installation as early as this afternoon. I agree and pay over the phone.

The phone rings and it's Cory Wainwright. He's around at his parents' place, continuing to sort through their stuff and says he's found something that might help with the investigation. He asks if I've got time to come over and have a look. I head over, leaving Quinn in charge of the office again. This is becoming a habit, and I'm not altogether uncomfortable with it.

At Cory's parents' house, he takes me into their den. Not many people have dens anymore, but Cory's parents did. It's a small room, lined with book-filled bookshelves, with an old mahogany roll-top desk and two leather reading chairs. Along one wall there are four large filing cabinets, all different colors and brands, obviously purchased at different times.

"I've been going through the filing cabinets," he sighs. "It's a nightmare. They kept everything. Both of them were serious hoarders but it's worked out well for our purposes. There are bank statements and bank books going back to before they were married. I've laid out the relevant ones on the desk."

I walk to the desk and start examining them as he explains.

"Here's a term investment for $150,000 that they terminated on September 17, three days after I was born. My father must have done it, obviously, as mom was confined to the hospital. Here's the bank book for their working account which shows the $150,000 going in. On the same day, they make two withdrawals from that same account. One for $120,000 in the form of a bank check and the other for $10,000 cash."

Cory looks at me. "That's how they paid for me."

It must be very strange and unsettling for him, to see these old transactions and contemplate the fact that he was purchased, like some kind of commodity.

"But that's not all," he continues. "There's a small safe in their wardrobe, and I've only just worked out how to get it open – it needed new batteries in the control pad. Inside, among other things, I found these."

He shows me three long-out-of-date passports; one each for his mother, his father and for him. His passport picture is of him as a newborn baby. The issue date for all three passports is September 17. The passports each have just two travel stamps in them; Monterrey International Airport, Mexico, on September 18, and San Jose International Airport, on September 20.

We stare at them together in silence for a moment, and then he says, quietly, "They got me from Mexico."

"Yes. They did," I agree. "It looks like they took the original baby down there with them and brought you back, all on the same passport."

"I don't understand," he says. "How could they possibly already have a passport for a baby when it's only a couple of days old?"

"They couldn't. The passport must be fake. And theirs were probably fake too, only because they needed them in a hurry."

"Fake passports? This is crazy! These are my boring parents we're talking about!"

"Yes. But sometimes ordinary people do crazy things when life deals them a difficult hand."

Cory is shaking his head, trying to take it all in.

"How are you coping?" I ask.

"I feel weird. Apparently, I'm a Mexican. I always thought my slightly olive skin and dark hair were some kind of genetic throw-back." He shakes his head, as if trying to shake all the pieces of the puzzle into a more sensible picture. "But how did my parents manage to organize it all so quickly?"

"There are several different scenarios that could have played out, Cory. Leave it with me. I'll keep investigating and try and get to the bottom of it for you. Now that we have this information, there's a possibility we might even be able to find where you came from. That's if you want me to continue."

"Yes. Of course. Please do. I want to find out."

I head back to the office soon after, with a bag of Cory's parents' bank records in my possession. I bring Quinn up to date and then we start brainstorming.

"I don't like the timing of it all," I say. "It's too tight. It doesn't actually work."

"How doesn't it work?" asks Quinn. "Cory is born on September 14. They get out of hospital on the 17th and fly to Mexico on the 18th. They spend a couple of days there and fly back with the new baby on the 20th."

"Yes, that's the easy part," I say. "It's the other stuff that doesn't work. They didn't get the laboratory test results indicating those terrible diseases until the 16th. That's when they found out they had a sick baby. But within two days, by the 18th, they've apparently tracked down and organized some kind of illicit baby swap in another country, bought fake passports, cancelled term deposits, had checks drawn up, booked plane flights and they're now sitting in a plane bound for Mexico. It's impossible that all that could have been arranged in just two days."

"So how do you explain it?" asked Quinn.

"There's really only one possible explanation."

"What?"

"Can you guess? Have a think about it. You say you're interested in a possible career as a PI. An important part of the job is solving puzzles. Let's see if you can work it out."

She thinks about it for a moment and shakes her head.

"I can't."

"I think you can. You're just not trying. Break it down into logical steps. How long do you reckon it would take to track down an illicit baby swap in another country, come to some sort of financial agreement and organize false passports?"

"I don't know. A few weeks, maybe. Possibly even a month or more."

"I agree. Even if there's some kind of agency that you can go to, who will organize all that for you, it will still all take time. So let's say a month."

"OK," she says, trying to see where I'm going with this.

"Good. Next question. Why did they decide to switch babies?"

"Because they found out their baby was very sick and they didn't want to care for it."

"Exactly. Now, here's the most important question. When did they find out that the baby was sick?"

"On the 16^(th)."

"You're answering the wrong question. That's when the testing laboratory – whatever it's called ..."

"California Laboratory for Neonatal Screening," she says, helpfully.

"Yes, that one. That's when the laboratory became aware of the baby's sickness as a result of neonatal testing and informed the *hospital*."

"Yes but ...," then she stops and thinks for a moment. Suddenly, the lights come on. "But the Wainwrights already knew! They'd already found out, somehow!"

"Yes. It's the only possible answer. They already knew their baby was going to be born with horrible diseases. That's how they managed to have everything so well organized, so that they basically left the hospital and hit the ground running."

"But how did they already know?"

"You can work that out too. How does anyone know that they have those kinds of diseases? What leads to the final, definitive diagnosis of any disease?"

"Medical tests?"

"Bingo! Yes. They must have had in-utero tests carried out sometime before the birth. Probably by their obstetrician."

"So, why bother having the tests done again after the baby was born?" she asks.

"Two reasons. Firstly, it wasn't their decision. Those are standard tests that are carried out on all newborn babies. The hospital would have done that as a matter of routine. Secondly, I've heard of cases of babies being wrongly diagnosed with various diseases in-utero and being born healthy. I'm guessing that the Wainwrights would have waited on the neonatal test results as a final confirmation of their baby's sickness, prior to transferring the money to whoever was helping them."

"So, how do we track down the original tests?"

"We won't bother. It's irrelevant to our investigation. What might be relevant is finding any kind of down-payment sometime prior to the birth. It's possible that they paid a deposit for the baby swap a month or so prior to the birth. The main payment of $120,000 was an untraceable bank check, but there's always the slim possibility that the down-payment was written out to a specific organization. And this is where I need your help."

I lift a large overnight bag from beside my desk and dump it on Quinn's desk.

"Here are all the Wainwright's bank records for the year of Cory's birth. Bank statements, bank passbooks, and check stubs. See if you can find a large payment to a strange organization a month or two prior to the birth."

She looks at the large bag of records with consternation.

"And what will you be doing, O Great and Glorious Leader?"

"I'm going to go for a pleasant walk in the sunshine."

"That's unfair! This is slavery."

"Well, as Leonidas the Great once said, 'Some of us are born to be great: the rest of you peasants have to put up with a lot of crap'."

"He did not! You just made that up!"

"Yep."

21

It took us two hours of tedious work to find an important piece of the puzzle. I took pity and helped look through the records, but in the end, it was Quinn who found it.

"Got it!" she exclaimed.

"What?" I say, looking up from a mound of bank statements, my eyes feeling bleary and heavy.

"A check stub, made out to Acorn Adoption Agency, for $40,000."

"Bingo! What date?"

"August 2. That's about six weeks before the birth."

"That sounds about right, in terms of both timing and amount. It brings the total payment for the baby swap to $160,000."

As Quinn starts typing on her keyboard, she asks, "So where did the Wainwrights get all this money from?"

"Cory says that his mother, Helen, was an only child. Her parents both died within a few months of each other about a year before Cory was born and she inherited a decent amount."

"Some people have all the luck!" she says, as she continues to type and click rapidly on her laptop keyboard.

"What are you doing?" I ask.

"I want to run a check on who actually owns Acorn."

As Quinn begins her research, a young guy arrives to install the security cameras. One of the cameras is a standard looking security camera that he attaches to the wall half-way up the stairs, pointing down into the entrance foyer. The second is a clock that he attaches to the office wall shared with the kitchen on the other side. We discuss the best place to install the hard drive recorder and decide to put it in one of the bottom kitchen cupboards below some power outlets. He installs a power cable down to the recorder and runs small cables from there to the two cameras, drilling through walls to do so. He then spends a few minutes configuring the system and shows me how to operate it. With his help I log on to the hard drive recorder from my own laptop, using Wi-Fi, and instantly I can see a split screen showing the empty foyer outside the office door and Quinn and I sitting at our desks in the office. The technician explains that the system is movement activated and has enough storage capacity to record continuously for 48 hours before it records back over the first data.

By the time he leaves, Quinn has made some further discoveries.

"Acorn Adoption Agency is actually owned by a parent company, called Pure Life Holdings, registered here in California."

"OK," I say.

"But here's where it gets interesting. Pure Life Holdings is the parent company for a whole bunch of other businesses apart from Acorn: Gentech Laboratories, a genetics R& D lab in Silicon Valley; New Life Health Spa, in Los Altos Hills; Pure Springs Health Spa, in Palm Springs; Little Blossom Adoption Agency, in LA."

"Wow! Impressive!"

"And here's the best bit," she continues. "Pure Life Holdings also owns five orphanages; two in El Salvador and three in Mexico."

"And let me guess; one of them is in Monterrey, Mexico, where the Wainwrights flew to?"

"You got it. It's called 'Casa de Gracia', the house of grace."

"So now we know where Cory came from; at least what orphanage he came from."

"So, what's the next step?" she asks.

"I don't suppose the orphanage has any kind of digital records that we can access?"

"Nope. I already checked. They've got a basic website asking for money, but that's about it."

"It's what I would expect. I'm guessing a place like that would have kept very minimal records, especially nearly thirty years ago."

"So, what do we do now?"

"That's up to Cory. We can tell him what orphanage he almost certainly came from, but if he wants to try to track down his origins any further than that, it would necessitate a trip to Monterrey. I'll contact him and see what he wants to do."

"So, what do you want me to do now?"

"To be honest, I don't think I've got anything for you at the moment. I've got two new cases from insurance companies, emailed to me overnight, that I haven't looked at yet. We can start on those on Monday. If you like, next week I'll be happy to take you out with me and teach you some basic surveillance skills. That's if you're interested in staying on."

"Does this mean I've passed my probation?"

"You've been incredibly helpful. I could definitely use your help on a regular basis, but I'm not sure I can offer you a regular salary. Someone with your skills could be out there earning big dollars and I just can't match that. The best I can offer at the moment is free board, paying your food bill, and

$100 on top of that. I'm sorry. I'll understand if you decide to try somewhere else."

"No. I think I'll stick around for a while longer. Especially if you're happy to teach me the practical side of investigation."

"Are you going to be able to manage, financially?"

"Yeah. I do wedding photography on the side. I get at least one gig each week, so I'm OK for cash."

"Great! It sounds like we've got a deal. Here's your first wage payment," I say, taking two fifties out of my wallet.

"No," she says, shaking her head. "The first week is on the house. That was our agreement. You can start paying me next week."

Quinn leaves soon after and I phone Cory. I tell him about the orphanage and ask him what he wants to do. He doesn't hesitate. He tells me he wants to go down there and see it for himself and he'll pay for me to accompany him. It looks like I'm going to Mexico.

22

———

The rest of the afternoon is a whirlwind of activity. If I'm going to Mexico for a few days I'm going to need to arrange for Addie to stay somewhere. Cory is keen to fly down to Monterrey as soon as possible, and is talking about booking flights for this Sunday, just two days' time. I know that Karl and Billie would gladly have Addie again, but I don't want to impose on them any further. After much thought I contact my ex-parents-in-law, Mortimer and Katherine. They are absolutely thrilled at the prospect of having Addie for a few days and thank me profusely for the opportunity. I get off the phone feeling guilty for my role in keeping Addie distant from them for so long.

Addie breezes in from school at 4:15, raids the kitchen for snacks, complains that we don't have 'anything decent' to eat, talks on the phone for almost an hour to a friend whom she is about to spend a whole night with anyway (go figure), and then rushes around packing her bag for the sleepover.

We leave at 5:45, stopping at a 7-Eleven on the way to buy snacks for the night's 'wake-over', as I prefer to call it. After dropping her off, I stop at a liquor store to buy a nice bottle of wine, as the restaurant I've booked is a BYO. By the time I get to Karl and Billie's it's 6:30 – right on time. The plan is for me to pick them up and drive them to the restaurant, so they can enjoy a few drinks without having to drive home. It's the least I can do for them after the way they've helped me this week. Billie opens the door and gives me a kiss and hug, but instead of inviting me inside, she steps out onto the front porch and closes the door behind her.

"John, I've been very naughty," she says with a guilty expression.

"What have you done?" I ask, although I have a suspicion that I know what she's about to say.

"I've cancelled the reservation and cooked dinner for us here."

"Oh, I see." It wasn't what I was expecting her to say. "For a moment I thought you were going to tell me that you'd lined me up with a date." I say it as a joke, but Billie grimaces and fixes me with an extremely apologetic face.

"Oh no, you have lined up a date!"

She nods. "I'm sorry."

"No you're not."

"You're right. I'm not. John, I think you're going to like her. She's absolutely lovely. I think she's perfect for you."

"No. I'm sorry, Billie. I'm not doing this. I want you to call her up and tell her you've made a mistake."

"Um ... that's a bit tricky. She's already here."

"She's inside?"

"Uh huh."

"Oh God, Billie! What have you done to me?" I run a hand through my hair in exasperation. "Besides, there's already someone else that I've ... well ... that I've decided to ask out."

She reaches out and touches my arm. "That's OK. You can still do that. This isn't a big deal. Just come in and have dinner. It won't kill you. And if, at the end of the night, you decide you're not interested, that's fine. You never have to see her again. This is just a low-key, relaxed meal. You can do this."

Without saying anything, I shake my head, turn around and walk toward the car.

"John! Come back, please! Where are you going?"

I stop and turn around.

"I'm getting the bottle of wine out of the car. I think I'm going to need it."

A minute later I brace myself and walk into their lounge room and stand there in stunned surprise. Claire Peters is sitting in a lounge chair staring at me with an equally shocked expression.

"Claire!" I say, completely dumbfounded.

She recovers quickly and flashes me one of her devastating smiles. "You really don't give up, do you?"

"You two know each other?" asks Karl, who is pouring some wine.

"You might say that," I answer.

"I stitched up his side, twice in two days."

"You're injured?" asks Billie.

"It's nothing," I say. "But how do you guys know each other?"

"Claire started coming to my book club a couple of months ago. She only lives two blocks away."

"Billie letter-boxed the local neighborhood, inviting people to the book club," explains Claire. "I saw the flyer and thought it would be a good way of meeting some people, as I'm new to the area."

"What kind of books do you like reading?" I ask, excited by the fact that we already share a common interest.

"I read quite widely across a range of genres."

"John has a PhD in English literature," says Billie, obviously hoping to market me as a more saleable commodity.

"I thought you said he was a soldier?"

"Ex-soldier," I clarify. "Now operating my own business – a small private investigation practice."

"I see," she says, regarding me with curiosity. "So, what kind of books do *you* like reading?"

"I read across a range of genres."

We both smile, and out of the corner of my eye I catch Billie and Karl exchanging a smug look.

Karl passes around the wine glasses and the three of us sit in the lounge room chatting, while Billie finishes setting the table.

"So, you didn't know it was me who was coming to dinner?" I ask.

"Billie just told me it was a good friend of Karl's from the army, called John."

"I'm not a strong believer in serendipity," I say, "but the chances of us meeting like this are pretty small."

Claire takes a sip of wine and says, "A wise person once said, 'serendipity is just God's way of remaining anonymous'."

"Who said that?"

"I can't remember, but I agree with the sentiment."

Billie soon calls us for dinner. She's gone to a lot of trouble. Clearly, she wants this matchmaking thing to work. There's some kind of fancy entrée with seafood, followed by beef cordon bleu with sautéed mushrooms and red wine jus. It's beautiful, but not as beautiful as the company. It's difficult to keep my eyes off Claire who is sitting opposite me looking absolutely lovely.

As we chat, I learn some of her story. Born and educated in England. Medical degree from University College London. Seven years working in the British hospital system. Broken engagement prompting a move to California. Five years at Los Angeles County Hospital, where she met, married and divorced her husband. Transferred to O'Connor Hospital, San Jose, two years ago.

"And you've just moved into the Santa Clara area recently?" I ask.

"Yes. I was renting near the hospital but felt like I wanted a quieter life in the suburbs."

"You two have a lot in common," says Billie, helpfully. "John lived in London when he was a boy."

"Really?" asks Claire. "I thought I detected a slight accent."

"Yes. Born in Australia. Then moved to London when I was ten and arrived in America when I was fifteen. Americans usually think I'm a Brit and Brits think I'm an Aussie."

"He also uses strange British words sometimes," adds Karl.

"What can I say? I'm a citizen of the world."

Karl then starts regaling her with stories from our time together at Los Alamitos and I do my best to keep him honest, as he has a tendency to exaggerate. Over coffee and dessert the talk turns to a variety of current affair topics, and I sense in Claire a sharp mind and a compassionate heart. I'm looking for boxes that aren't being ticked, but I'm not finding any. Toward the end of the evening, Claire asks me about Addie. Perhaps it's the two glasses of red wine I've drunk, but I find myself opening up about my feelings of inadequacy as a father.

"You love her very much," Claire says. It's a statement, not a question.

"She's my whole world," I say, choking up as tears fill my eyes. I clear my throat. "I just wish I knew what the hell I was doing. I'm making it up as I go along."

"I think we're all doing that," she says.

Soon afterward, Claire decides it's time to leave and I offer to drive her home.

"Let's walk," she responds. "It's a nice night."

We thank my friends for a lovely evening and we stroll side by side along the sidewalk. There is a three-quarter moon intermittently breaking through light wispy clouds and even though the air is cool, it holds a fragrant hint of the coming spring. I really want to reach out and take her hand, but I don't want to act too prematurely and frighten her away.

All too soon, we reach her front gate and we stop.

"Well, this is me."

"It looks like a nice place."

"It's all I need for the moment."

We stand looking at each other and there is an awkward silence.

"I was going to ask you out," I say.

"I thought you'd decided not to."

"Well, I was working myself up to it. I wasn't sure you were interested."

"You weren't sure? I thought I was putting out enough signals to make contact with a satellite in space."

"My radar's a bit defective. It's been out of action for a few years."

I notice a puff of breeze blow a wisp of hair across her face. I'd love to reach out and touch her. My heart is thumping now.

"Would you mind if I kissed you?"

Her face suddenly turns severe. "I'd like to see you try."

I take an involuntary step backward. "Sorry. I just thought …"

"John," she says, reaching out to hold my hand. "I'm teasing you. I actually mean it. I'd really like to see you try." She gives me a cheeky smile.

I lean forward and tenderly caress her lips with mine. After a few moments, I pull away and look at her. She raises her eyebrows and tilts her head slightly to the side.

"Not bad. But I think you can do a whole lot better."

This time I draw her into my arms and I am lost in the softness of her mouth and the sweetness of her breath. I don't want it to end, but eventually we break apart.

"Mm," she says with a sigh. "Not bad for a Doctor of Literature."

"I can also kiss like a soldier, if you're interested."

"Whoah, there, tiger! One step at a time," she says, leaning in to give me a peck on the cheek. "Goodnight."

As she walks down the path to her front door, I ask, "When can I see you again?"

She stops and turns.

"I don't know. When would you like to?"

"How about every day for the rest of my life?"

"Is that a line you use on every girl?"

"I'm trying it out on you first, to see how it works."

She laughs.

"Let's just start with tomorrow. How about you come over for lunch? You can bring your daughter."

"Sounds great."

"It won't be anything special. Just homemade soup and rolls, probably."

"Sounds doubly great."

"OK, well I'll see you around midday. Goodnight, John."

"Goodnight, Claire."

23

I'm still on cloud nine the next morning as I drive to the YMCA to set up for the third and final lesson for this current class. Jimmy, at the front desk, greets me and informs me that the management committee has agreed to the purchase of three more dummies, which will enable me to have an additional six people in a class, thereby doubling the class size. The dummies will arrive within the next week and will be ready for the Tuesday night classes that will start in ten days' time.

I quickly set up the mats and dummies and greet the women as they arrive. We spend the first ten minutes going over the skills from the previous two weeks. Firstly, I get them to practice the three responses when grabbed from behind; reverse head butt, elbow strike, and heel rake with foot stomp. Then they practice the responses to a frontal assault: head butt, upward palm strike to the nose, and the three variations of the nut strikes.

"Remember," I recap, "the particular nut strike you use will depend on how far away from the attacker you are. If you're far enough away to do a full-blooded kick, go for it! That's the nut smasher. If you're being held close, use your knee; the nut-cracker. And if you are being held very close, or held down, reach out and grab with your hand and squeeze as hard as you can; the nut masher."

I move on to today's lesson; escape techniques when being restrained. The two issues I focus on now are escaping from a headlock and escaping from an arm grab. We do one at a time, with me demonstrating the technique several times first, and then the women practicing on each other. Once again, I am impressed with their enthusiasm and aggression, and I walk around the class correcting techniques and giving individual encouragement.

The final five minutes of the class are spent with me giving them a pep talk about prevention as the best form of defense. I give them a handout of safety tips, dealing with simple steps such as never walking alone at night and avoiding unlit areas, as well as tips suggested by the police such as carrying a whistle, pepper spray, intimidating with your scream and running before it's too late. I say to them that it's better to run screaming and yelling away from someone and be wrong, than to be too embarrassed to act and end up dead.

The class ends with a round of applause and I have a feeling of satisfaction that I may have helped save someone's life. As the women thank me one by one and leave, Asha, the barbie-doll blonde, hands me her card and touches my arm intimately, saying, "Call me sometime, John. I'd really like to see you." She walks out the door, doing her best to strut her stuff.

I finish packing up and as I walk past the front desk, I hand Jimmy the card from Asha.

"Hey Jimmy. The hot blonde in that class gave me her card and asked me to give it to you. She wants you to call her."

"No shit?"

"Yeah. I think she's got the hots for you, man."

"Thanks dude!"

"No problem."

As I drive home, I'm thinking about lunch with Claire when I realize I've made a major blunder. I'd completely forgotten about Addie's soccer match. She's playing at 12:30 today! We can't possibly go to Claire's for lunch. I also realize that I don't have Claire's phone number. I pull over and call Billie, who is more than happy to give me Claire's number. Claire answers after a couple of rings.

"Claire, it's John."

"John who?"

"John Targett."

"John Targett?" she says, sounding confused.

"Um ... yeah ... you know ... the guy who kissed you last night."

"Let me see ...," she says vaguely. "Last night ... Oh yes, I've got a vague recollection. You might have to refresh my memory when I see you again."

I could seriously fall in love with this woman.

"I'll definitely take you up on that offer. But listen, I've made a major boo-boo."

"A boo-boo? Sounds serious. In fact, I haven't encountered any kind of boo-boo, either major or minor, for many years. Are you sure you're from this century?"

"Well, my daughter is certainly convinced I'm not. And it's actually about her that I'm calling. I completely forgot that Addie has an earlier soccer match today. She's playing at 12:30."

"Oh, I see."

"I'm so sorry."

"Do you normally eat lunch before soccer?"

"Not when she plays this early."

"Then why don't you come back here for a late lunch after soccer?"

"Are you sure that's not too much trouble. It'll be nearly 2:30 by the time we get to your place."

"It's no trouble."

Then I get an inspiration.

"Actually, I've got another idea. How about you come to soccer with us? Then we'll head back to your place after. That's if you want to. I'll totally understand if you think that's a bit too much, too soon."

She seems to be hesitating, so I try some emotional manipulation.

"To be honest, I could really use your protection. There are two single soccer moms who have been chasing me up and down the sideline for weeks. It's exhausting."

I can hear her laughing, now. "OK, it's a deal."

"Great, I'll pick you up at 11:45."

...

The timing is tight. Addie gets home from the 'wake-over' at 10:45 and we are out the door again by 11:30, heading to Claire's. She is ready as soon as we get there, and she gets into the car wearing tight black jeans, a cream buttoned shirt and a black jacket. She makes it all look like a million dollars.

Introductions are made as we drive to the ground across town and Claire makes an instant connection with Addie. When Addie discovers that Claire is a doctor, they quickly become engrossed in a discussion about sexually transmitted infections, which is the topic of her health assignment due next week. They spend the entire trip speaking about genital herpes, vaginal discharge and cervical warts. I feel as though I have slipped into some kind of weird alternate reality. By the time we get to the ground they appear to have forgotten that I was in the car at all and seem vaguely surprised to see me.

As we walk toward the patch of grass where her team has dumped their gear, Addie turns to Claire and asks, "Are you Dad's girlfriend now?"

"Addie!" I say, somewhat embarrassed. "That's not the sort of direct question you ask someone."

Addie ignores me and continues to address Claire.

"It's OK if you're not. But if you're thinking about it, just bear in mind that he hasn't got a clue about women."

"Well, I must have some sort of clue," I interject, mortally offended. "I managed to produce you, didn't I? I certainly didn't harvest you from a pumpkin patch."

"That's just the physical stuff, Dad. I'm talking about picking up women's signals." She turns to Claire again. "He really needs help. I'm worried about him."

Claire smiles at her affectionately.

"Thanks for the tip. I'll do my best."

As Addie joins her teammates, I see YM1 and YM2 heading in my direction. They've locked on with their radar and their missiles are armed and ready for launch.

"Oh Lord, here come the yummy mommies. Do something, Claire. Help!"

She reaches up and gives me a long, lingering kiss, then slips her arm through mine and snuggles up beside me.

"How's that? Any good?"

"Brilliant! Absolutely bloody brilliant! Although it might need to be repeated at regular intervals to keep them at bay."

"I'll see what I can do."

It's the first win of the season and most of the parents can hardly believe it. Addie scores two goals and is the star of the game, and I'm sure my regularly shouted instructions are the main factor in her brilliant performance. Claire seems mildly amused at my soccer enthusiasm. I must remember to sit her down sometime and explain to her the finer points of game strategy.

Claire's presence has done the trick. The single moms have powered down their heat-seeking missiles and have resumed scanning the horizon for other suitable targets. Addie notices it too, and as we leave the ground, she makes a facetious comment about how I've broken two hearts today.

We spend the entire afternoon and early evening at Claire's. Soup for lunch and toasted sandwiches for dinner, interspersed with a game of Monopoly, a walk to the corner store to get an ice cream and a re-run of Notting Hill. I try to put on a macho image as the movie starts, but Addie spills the beans and tells Claire that it's one of my favorite films. Claire and I watch it cuddled up on the lounge together, with Addie sprawled across the floor, providing us with various interjections of hilarious commentary.

As we leave, Addie says she'll wait for me in the car, giving me a few moments alone with Claire. I try to assure Claire that the yummy mommies are no longer in the immediate vicinity, but she spends several minutes continuing to implement the protective strategies that she commenced at the game, 'just to be sure'.

As I lie in bed later that night, a feeling of euphoria persists. Something that I thought was dead inside me has come to life. And I think I'm falling for Claire.

24

The plane touches down at Monterrey International Airport at 4:15 pm local time. I dropped Addie at Mort and Katherine's a little after eight this morning, and Cory and I have had a long day of travel since then, including a two-hour layover at Houston while we waited for a connecting flight.

I used the time to do some research into the state of orphanages in Mexico, and what I discovered shocked me to the core. Orphanages in Mexico operate under an almost complete absence of government oversight and supervision. There are no official regulations governing their operation and no system of inspections or accountability. As a result, there is widespread abuse and violations of basic human rights within many orphanages. Children live in squalid conditions, in buildings infested with cockroaches and rats, and there are regular reports of children being raped, beaten and forced to beg in the streets. Some orphanages are run by the Mexican underworld, and in these cases, children are abducted from their homes and held against their wills in the hope of selling them to rich foreigners looking to adopt a child. There are over seven hundred known orphanages in Mexico, housing forty thousand children. Numerous attempts by the United Nations to apply pressure to the Mexican government to clean up the sector have so far failed.

But that's not the end of the story. Twelve thousand babies are orphaned, deserted or abducted in Mexico every year and about ten thousand of those are never located. No doubt, some are killed. But many become commodities in the booming baby trade for Americans looking to buy a baby illegally. Light-skinned babies are at particular risk and are a common target for crime syndicates who specialize in the baby trade.

The more I read, the less confident I am that we will find Cory's origins. Perhaps the best we can hope for is to visit the orphanage and return home with the assurance that he was one of the lucky ones, to have escaped a life of misery and abuse.

On the final leg of our journey, I continue my research. There is a reason why the Mexican government is powerless to regulate orphanages; Mexico is ruled by crime syndicates. Monterrey, our destination, is the home territory of one of the country's most notorious crime gangs; La Fraternidad, 'The Brotherhood'. It is a vast and highly regimented organization that resembles the military, with varying ranks of officers and foot soldiers. They operate openly and brazenly, ruling the city. They even advertise in local papers for recruits, attracting ex-soldiers and ex-police to their ranks because they offer much higher pay. In recent years, La Fraternidad has been responsible for attacks on casinos and police stations who refused to pay the protection money that was demanded.

After we land at Monterrey, Cory and I grab a taxi and head south-west into the city. The city is a strange mixture of poverty and affluence. The outskirts are dominated by trash-laden streets with cinder block two room shanties. As we enter the city, the shanties give way to more substantial homes. We drive past fast-food outlets, airconditioned shopping malls and a visual collage of gaudily decorated entertainment venues, offering anything from girls to gambling. We're booked into a hotel on the other side of town, a couple of blocks from the Casa de Gracia orphanage. The hotel Casa de Paz, 'the house of peace,' is ancient and faded, with barely-adequate rooms. Perhaps the reason it's peaceful is that it's so run-down that no one stays here anymore, but at least it's within walking distance of the orphanage.

After dumping our bags in our adjoining ground floor rooms, we decide we may as well pay the orphanage a visit. We take our time walking the two blocks, with Cory looking intently around him, coming to terms with his origins. The suburb is a big improvement on the shanties on the periphery of the city, but it is still relatively squalid by western standards. There are rows of identical, white-painted concrete houses with red tiled roofs, squashed alongside each other with barely room to walk between. Children are sitting in the gutters and playing soccer in the street with some kind of a lumpy home-made soccer ball, and we can't walk far without being accosted and asked for money.

We reach the orphanage. It consists of three buildings, all painted bright blue, arranged in a 'U' around a central, concreted courtyard. The building at the top of the 'U' is two storied, and the two on the sides are single story. There is a six-foot brick wall enclosing the whole complex and the only access is via a double-gated entry, wide enough to allow a vehicle. Spanning the entry is a curved metal framework with a battered sign; 'Casa de Gracia'. The gates are currently open and there are at least eighty children in the courtyard, playing soccer and other games.

"It looks like it used to be a school," observes Cory.

"Yes. But there's a lot more money in selling children than educating them."

We stop at the entrance, uncertain whether to proceed any

further, because leaning against one of the open gates is a guard in militia uniform with an AR-15 assault rifle slung casually over his shoulder. He stubs his cigarette out and takes a step toward us.

"Who are you and what do you want?" he says in heavily accented English. He's obviously summed us up as Americans.

"We want to speak to someone about a child." It's not a lie, but the child I'm speaking about was here twenty-nine years ago and is standing in front of him right now.

He looks us up and down, perhaps estimating our wealth.

"Show me some ID."

I flash him my American driver's license and he stares at it carefully for a few seconds then flicks his head, indicating that we can enter.

"Straight ahead, in the office." He's lost interest in us even before we've walked past him, and he lights another cigarette as he resumes the important task of propping up the gate.

"Let me do the talking," I say to Cory as we walk across the courtyard.

The children largely ignore us as we walk through their games, apparently used to such visitors. They are dressed shabbily, and there are no shoes in sight, but they don't appear to be starving.

We walk through the open door marked 'Oficina' with the English translation, 'Office', helpfully provided underneath. It is a small square room, with a door on the far wall opening into a corridor beyond. Paint is peeling from the walls and the floor is aged concrete, stained and pitted from decades of wear. There are two rickety wooden chairs against the left wall and a drab counter running almost the length of the far wall, ending just short of the doorway. A grimy telephone sits forlornly on the bench behind the counter, and a small desk fan is rhythmically clicking and groaning as it pushes warm air around.

The counter is unattended, so I call out, "Hello! Anyone there?"

Moments later a young woman in a black skirt and a gaudily-colored top walks through the door.

"Yes? What do you want?" She doesn't exactly exude friendliness.

"I am interested in adopting a baby," I say.

"For you?"

"Yes. For me and my wife."

"Si. We can do this for you." Her manner has changed now, as she sees the potential dollar value in me.

"How long will it take?"

"Adoption process in Mexico is very, very slow. It takes many months, with much paperwork."

"I don't want to wait many months, and I don't want to fill out any paperwork."

She seems suddenly very cautious. She looks at me carefully.

"Is such a thing possible?" I ask.

She nods. "Si. It is possible. But there is a great cost involved."

"How much?"

"That is not for me to say. Mamá Rosa is in charge of special orders."

"Can I speak with her?"

"Mamá Rosa is not here now. You come back tomorrow. Three o'clock. Bring passport."

"Do you keep records of your special orders?"

She looks at me as if I am stupid.

"No records for special orders. You come back tomorrow."

There seems little point in having any further discussion. We retrace our steps through the games of the children and out past the chain-smoking guard. As we walk back toward our hotel, Cory says what we are both thinking.

"It looks like there's zero chance of finding out anything more about my origins."

"I'm afraid so, Cory. There won't be any records of illegal transactions like this."

Cory continues to gaze around him, soaking up his surroundings.

"I was born somewhere here. Taken from my parents. From my brothers and sisters and aunties and uncles."

"Not necessarily taken," I comment. "There are plenty of poor families who can't afford contraception and who are willing to sell their babies for money. There's a thriving baby economy here that some families rely on for their survival. The sale of a single baby can keep a whole family fed for a year or more."

"It doesn't seem fair," says Cory.

"None of it's fair," I agree. "But you might have to console yourself with the thought that both you and your birth family were much better off as a result of your 'adoption'."

"I wasn't expecting to see an armed guard at an orphanage," Cory comments.

"It's a clear sign that it's run by a crime gang. Probably La Fraternidad."

"But I thought we'd already discovered that the orphanage is owned by a company in California, linked to Acorn Adoption Agency."

"It is. But this is how things operate in Mexico. The crime syndicates have their fingers in every part of the economy. They're probably scooping fifty percent of the profits from the orphanage."

"It's a partnership made in hell," says Cory.

"It is indeed."

We keep walking, past our hotel toward the center of the city, deciding to look for somewhere to eat. We bypass a lot of shady-looking diners and takeouts that look like they serve deep-fried bacteria, and finally come to a restaurant that seems to cater to tourists. We walk through the impressively arched entrance of the Casagrande and are quickly given a table. After filling our plates from the large buffet bar we discuss what tomorrow might bring.

"Is there any point even going back tomorrow?" asks Cory. "If there aren't any records, there's nothing more we can find out."

"Nothing more we can find out about you," I agree. "But I'd like to know what happened to the original Cory. Your parents arrived here with him but left with you. Where did he go?"

"I've got a bad feeling about what might have happened to him," says Cory.

"So have I."

25

———

Mamá Rosa is a formidable-looking character. She is well into her sixties, with almost pure white hair and a deeply lined face, complete with a tattoo on one cheek. Some kind of symbol. But it's her eyes that capture me; they are intelligent and cold, and I get the feeling that she can peer into my soul. She sits us down in two padded chairs and walks around to take her seat on the other side of her desk. My mobile phone is recording the entire conversation.

"So! You would like to adopt a baby? Is that correct?" Her English is perfect, with almost no trace of an accent.

"Yes. And my wife and I are prepared to bypass the usual legal formalities."

"I see." She stares at me for a few moments. "Let me see your passport."

I hand it over, and she looks at it carefully. She holds a stamped page up to the light and looks through it, then nods, satisfied, and hands it back.

"Good. We can do business. Where are you staying?"

Cory answers before I have a chance to make up a name. "Casa de Paz."

"And who are you?" she says, looking at him.

"He's just a friend," I respond. "My wife couldn't make it this trip."

She returns her attention to me. "What kind of baby do you want? How old?"

"We want a newborn. No more than one month. And white skinned."

"That will be very expensive."

"How much?"

"$60,000 U.S." She stars at me intently. "$20,000 as a deposit and the rest on delivery."

I nod, showing her that I'm unfazed. "There is another complication."

"Yes?"

"My wife is pregnant, and the baby has a serious genetic disease. We want to ... shall we say ... exchange it."

"I see."

"Can you do it?"

"An extra $20,000. Upfront."

"How does the exchange work? Does it take place here?"

"No. We have a facility, in the hills to the north. We will give you the address at the right time."

"And what happens to the sick baby?"

"We take care of it."

"What do you mean?"

"It will not suffer; I promise you that."

"You dispose of it?"

"We live in a strange world, do we not?" she says. "We shoot horses and put down animals when they are sick and suffering, but we prolong the agony of humans when there is no possibility of any quality of life."

"You kill it?" asks Cory, unable to contain himself. "You murder an innocent child, for money!"

Mamá Rosa looks at Cory then addresses me. "Your friend is uncomfortable with our proposed arrangements. Perhaps it is better that we don't proceed."

"Uncomfortable? I'm more than uncomfortable! I'm sickened! My life was purchased at the cost of another innocent life!" Cory is visibly shaking now. The full import of his origins has overwhelmed him with a mixture of guilt and anger. I realize too late that it was a bad idea to bring him with me today.

"I'm sorry. My friend is not well," I say, standing. "I'll come back another time so we can conclude the arrangements."

Mamá Rosa is glaring at us, with eyes that have closed to mere slits. A dark expression has clouded her features, and she speaks now with a menacing tone. "You didn't come here to adopt a baby." It's a statement, not a question. "I think it would be best if you don't come back at all."

We make a hasty retreat and as we walk quickly back to our hotel, Cory is deeply remorseful.

"I'm so sorry! I completely lost it in there. I just can't bear the thought of what they did back then."

As we hurry back to the hotel, he starts to think through the implications of what he just did.

"Shit! Are we in trouble?"

"Possibly. It might be a good idea to change hotels. Immediately."

We get back to the hotel and order a taxi. Our bags are packed within a few minutes and our bill is finalized. The taxi arrives soon after, and we ask to be taken to a hotel close to the airport. We check in to a well-known hotel chain and are given adjoining rooms on the fourth floor, with balconies overlooking a rear garden. Cory has been practically wetting himself with fear, but I tell him to calm down.

"We're safe now. They can't find us here. Relax."

"Do you think they might go looking for us?" asks Cory.

I don't want to frighten him, but I'm not going to lie.

"It's possible. Mamá Rosa is almost certainly a member of the criminal gang operating the orphanage, and she saw straight through us. She doesn't know who we are, exactly, but she may suspect that we are from some sort of anti-crime agency or government department. She might even think we're CIA. I don't know. But one thing I do know; Mexican gangs don't tolerate people snooping into their activities."

"Can they find us here?"

"I doubt it. We didn't tell anyone where we were going, and we left straight away. I'm pretty sure we're safe now."

"I'm so sorry!" he says again, running his hand through his hair.

I open the mini-bar and pull out a beer.

"Here. Drink this."

He shakes his head. "I think I need something stronger."

He grabs a min-bottle of Johnny Walker, cracks it and takes a long gulp.

"Sorry," he says again.

"It's OK. No damage done. What time is our flight tomorrow?"

"I booked the early one. 7:10 am."

"That'll do fine."

As Cory finally starts to relax, I grab my mobile phone and replay the recording of our conversation with Mamá Rosa. My voice is clear and strong. Mamá Rosa's is much fainter and very muffled, but her words can still be distinguished. I save the file to the cloud and send a copy to my office email address.

I'm feeling a little stale, so I take the opportunity to work out in the hotel gym, while Cory continues to soothe his nerves with further medicinal whisky. By 6:00, Cory has calmed down and I'm feeling refreshed and energized after a good workout and a shower. We head downstairs to eat dinner in the hotel restaurant, enjoying perfectly cooked steaks. As we eat, Cory reflects on what we've learned today.

"From what you and your assistant discovered from my parents' accounts, they paid a total of $160,000 for me, nearly thirty years ago, but these people were only going to charge $80,000 in total for a baby swap. What's with that?"

"American greed and profiteering," I explain. "The orphanage down here probably charged even less thirty years ago, maybe $40,000. So Acorn Adoption Agency were probably quadrupling the charge, taking advantage of desperate parents."

Cory shakes his head. "This whole thing is surreal. I'm finding it hard to come to terms with."

"I'm sure you are."

"These people are murdering babies, and American parents are paying them to do it! It's ... it's ... heinous!"

"What do you want to do about it?"

"What do you mean? What can I do?"

"Well, you've got two choices," I explain. "On the one hand, you could do nothing. You could go home, resume your life, and be thankful for the chance you've been given. On the other hand, we could try to bring these people to justice."

"How?"

"We could approach the FBI. Obviously, they have no jurisdiction in Mexico, but with the evidence we've accumulated, it could be enough for indictments to be issued for the American side of the operation."

"Is there a down-side to option two? Would it place me in danger?"

"The only risk would be if you were called to testify, but I can't see that happening, as you are effectively a piece of evidence, rather than an eyewitness to a crime. So, no, I don't think you would be in any real danger."

Cory takes a sip of his beer and stares into the glass.

"These people can't be allowed to keep getting away with this."

"No. They can't," I agree.

26

———————

I've always been a big believer in the philosophy, 'Hope for the best; prepare for the worst'. My time in the army, particularly officer training school, taught me to never underestimate the enemy and always have a number of possible response plans in mind.

As far as I know, we are safe in our new hotel. We moved here quickly and told no one of our new digs. On the other hand, the orphanage was clearly being run by a criminal organization, probably La Fraternidad, and gangs like that tend to react very aggressively if they feel they are under any kind of surveillance. I am also aware that La Fraternidad rules the city, with contacts and connections in almost every major business and industry in Monterrey. There is a slim chance that they may be able to track us down. I think we're safe, but I'm not prepared to bet my life on it.

Before I go to bed, I make a few preparations. I balance a plastic coat hanger on the door handle, resting it across the top of the handle with its edge leaning against the side wall. Any attempt to open the door will send the coat hanger tumbling to the wooden floor in the entrance. I also place two spare pillows under the bed sheet down the left side of the bed, closest to the balcony, making it look like a sleeping body. Finally, I find the best weapon in the room, a metal corkscrew with a wooden handle, and place it on the nightstand. Hope for the best; prepare for the worst.

It's a balmy night and I leave the glass sliding door of our fourth-floor balcony wide open to let in a fresh breeze. I've never been a big fan of air-conditioning. The moon is hidden behind clouds tonight, but the lights of the city put on a dazzling display. In the distance I can see the green lasers from the Faro de Comercio tower shooting up into the sky and tracing eerie patterns on the undersides of clouds. I lay on the right side of the bed alongside the line of pillows and closest to the en suite, watching the city lights and listening to the sounds of a city that never sleeps.

Eventually, I fall asleep and the next thing I am aware of is the sound of the coat hanger falling to the floor with a clatter. I am a very light sleeper and I am instantly on my feet with the corkscrew in my hand, and a moment later I step into the en suite. I just make it inside before the door opens and the light from the hallway cuts a wedge into the darkness of the room. The door closes silently, which tells me that whoever is now in the room is being careful. There is no sound now. The intruder is standing perfectly still. Not moving. Barely breathing. Listening. Waiting. He's a professional. Not rushing. Taking his time to assess for danger. I stand equally still, listening and waiting.

He is standing in the tiny entrance hall, on the other side of the en suite wall, so he can't yet see the bed. He must have heard the coat hanger fall but probably doesn't attribute anything sinister to it. He's just trying to assess whether the sound woke me. We are standing only a few feet apart, separated by the en suite wall, both of us silent, listening. I have slowed my breathing down, but I'm taking deep, long lung-fulls of air with each breath, trying to super-oxygenate my blood.

We continue to stand in silence and the longer it lasts the more I realize that I am dealing with a professional. He is listening for the slightest sound that might indicate that I am awake and alert. He will be armed and I'm not, but I have one advantage: I know that he's there and he doesn't know that I know.

The silence lasts for at least two full minutes. He's very good. Finally, I hear the faintest breath and a slight rustle of material as he begins to move. A moment later there is the unmistakable 'phut phut' of a silenced pistol and the dull impacts as the bullets penetrate the pillows. The next few seconds are crucial. They will determine whether he lives or dies. If he leaves the room now, he will believe that I am dead. If he switches a light on, he will see my deception and I will have to kill him.

There is a faint click and a torch beam lights up the bed and as it does, I burst from the open en suite. His torch is swinging toward me now and everything seems to happen in slow motion as my adrenaline surges and the instinctual muscle movements take over. He is right-handed, which is hindering him because I'm coming at him from the left and his gun hand has further to travel and his left hand is in the way now because he's still holding the torch. His eyes have also momentarily lost their night vision because he was staring along the light beam but I was anticipating it, looking away from the bed. I throw the towel that I've had in my hand toward his gun and it arcs across the torch beam like a white ghost and drapes his gun. There is the soft 'phut' of another round being fired but it is wide and I'm inside his arc of fire now and I punch him in the throat with a savage roundhouse left. He drops the gun and the torch simultaneously and staggers backward, lifting his hands to his damaged throat. He can't help it; it's instinctual, because the urge to breathe is the body's strongest urge and when it is compromised, the psyche focuses all its energy on that one urgent need. My punch has probably ruptured his thyroid cartilage, as well as traumatized his hypoglossal nerve, and I can see his eyes bulging in the dim light as he gasps for breath. But the fight hasn't completely left him. He is clearly a professional because a moment later there is a knife in his hand and he assumes a classic attack stance and stops panicking because he realizes that he can still draw enough air to survive.

He sees the corkscrew in my right hand and notes my stance, sensing that he is not facing an amateur. We circle each other warily, both of us feinting and lunging to test the other. In the light from the torch on the floor our shadows dance around the walls as if in some kind of macabre mating ritual. I look for the gun but can't see it. It must be just under the edge of the bed.

I need to get to the balcony so I can use the corkscrew without making a mess on the carpet. It's why I didn't use it in my first attack, otherwise he'd already be dead. I lunge and retreat and he does the same, and I edge further around to my left. He feints to my right and then comes at me suddenly with a series of lightning strikes that I only just manage to avoid. But I've reached the open balcony door now, and I retreat backward, out through the door. I note the gleam of triumph in his eyes because he thinks he's got me: I've got nowhere to go. He shifts his hand grip on the knife slightly, probably unconsciously, but it signals what he is about to do. I encourage him further by subtly angling my wrist as I'm holding the corkscrew and shifting my weight as if I'm preparing for a backhand strike.

He comes at me then, greedy for the opening that I've given him, lunging too quickly, but I'm already pivoting, and as his knife slices thin air to my left I drive the corkscrew into the side of his neck and rip it out, twice in rapid succession, two lightning strikes that take less than half a second, then I step away as he tries to slice me across my back and misses. He is staggering now, and blood is pumping out of his neck and coursing down his chest. By the color of the blood, I've severed both his jugular vein and carotid artery. Blood pressure to the brain is now plummeting and he drops his knife as he falls to his knees.

I leave him there and quickly move back into the bedroom. I pick up the gun and check that it still has rounds in it and that the safety isn't on. I need to check that there isn't a second assailant for Cory. I cautiously open the door between our rooms. Cory is snoring peacefully.

By the time I return to the balcony the assassin is dead. It's the first time I've killed someone, but I don't feel remorse. Perhaps I should. But the reality is that as soon as he walked into my room tonight, one of us was going to die. I had no choice. If I had merely incapacitated him, or put him in hospital, Cory and I would probably not get out of the country alive. My response had to be deadly and final.

I've already thought through how I will dispose of the body. It can't be found until we are out of the country and I certainly can't call the police, because they are basically owned by the crime gangs. I check the time. 3:20 am. Perfect. There will be no one around. I look over the balcony and check the garden and the grounds below, then lift the body and let it topple over the balcony. It falls four floors and lands with a thud in a garden bed of palms and exotic plants.

I quickly wash my hands and arms and grab my key. I slept in my clothes, so there is no need to get changed. I step out into the empty corridor and take the fire stairs down to the ground floor. They open onto a small vestibule out of view of the reception desk. My room key-card also opens the rear door into the garden and I quietly walk out into the mild night air. The hotel gardens and lawn end in a metal fence, beyond which there is a densely wooded hill. It's why I chose this hotel. I retrieve the body and hoist it across my shoulders. It takes me twenty minutes to 'lug the guts', as Shakespeare would say. I find a shallow ditch on the far side of the hill and cover the body in leaves and rotting branches. With any luck it will be days before the body is discovered. I bury the knife and gun separately from the body, wiping them carefully to remove fingerprints.

The clean-up in the room takes longer. Countless trips back and forth to the bathroom are required in order to mop up the blood on the balcony with a wet towel. It is almost an hour before I'm finished. Two pillows have holes in them and although they aren't obvious, I stick them up the top of the wardrobe and replace them with another two. It's the first time I've been thankful for hotel rooms providing a ridiculous number of pillows. I can't do anything about the bullet holes in the bed and sheets but to an untrained eye they look like cigarette burns. There is an obvious bullet hole in the wall to the right and just above the en suite door. I carefully patch that with toothpaste and then stand back to examine it from a distance. You can only notice it if you stare at it. I wash the towel that I mopped the balcony with, using hot water and shampoo, and it cleans up pretty well. I leave it wet in the bath. It also has a hole in it. Nothing I can do about that either.

By the time I've finished it's 4:50 am and I hear Cory's alarm going off in the next room. A moment later he knocks on our mutual door and opens it.

"Just checking you're up. We need to leave in fifteen minutes." He looks at me carefully. "You look like shit. Did you have a bad night?"

"I've had better."

27

I decide not to tell Cory about our overnight visitor. He's scared enough as it is. In fact, I will never tell anyone. This is something I will have to live with for the rest of my life.

As we sit in the taxi on the way to the airport, I try to work out how they found us. It was either the taxi driver or the concierge. Either way, it shows the ubiquitous reach of La Fraternidad and also demonstrates how quickly and aggressively they are prepared to act when they feel that one of their lucrative businesses is threatened. When I searched the assassins' pockets last night, I found two hotel room keys, and the only way he could have obtained them was from the concierge. I left the keys in one of the desk drawers.

I had deliberately chosen the room closest to the elevators, and I was fairly confident that if they sent someone for us, they would go to my room first. But just in case I was wrong, before I went to bed I had sneaked into Cory's room while he was snoring and wedged a chair under his door handle. If the assassin had gone to his room first it would have made enough noise to wake us both.

As we stand in line at the check-in, I try to think if there is any way La Fraternidad can reach us once we are home. I am confident they can't. We gave false home addresses at both hotels, and Mamá Rosa's brief examination of my passport would not have been enough for her to memorize my home address.

Once we've checked our bags in and have been through the security station, we have over an hour to kill and I'm starving. The emotional and physical expenditure from last night's activities has kicked in and my body is craving food. We grab a table at a food outlet and I order a full fry up with the works.

"Wow!" says Cory, who has settled for a breakfast bagel and a coffee. "You sure worked up a big appetite overnight."

If only he knew.

It's another long day of travel and I spend most of it sleeping. The one bright moment is a phone call from Claire while we are on a layover at Houston. We've been texting back and forth over the last couple of days.

"Hi," she says.

"Who is this?"

"It's Claire."

"Claire who?"

"Ha ha. It's not as funny the second time around. Besides, you're stealing my material."

"What are you up to at the moment?" I ask.

"Not much. I'm on an early lunch break and I'm bored, so I thought I'd give you a call."

"I'm very happy to be your boredom reliever, any time you need me."

"It could become a regular thing."

"Regular is good."

"I really enjoyed having you and Addie over on Saturday."

"Same."

"She's a delightful girl, John, and she clearly loves you to bits. I think you're doing a great job raising her."

I must be tired, because my eyes well up with tears as she says this. I clear my throat.

"She was pretty impressed with you, as well," I say, after a moment. "Apparently you're 'really nang for an oldie'. I think that's a compliment."

"Where are you now?" she asks.

"Houston. We've got another half hour until they call our flight."

There's a moment's silence between us.

"What are you doing tonight?" I ask. "Is there any chance you might be bored?"

"Very."

"That's handy, because I was thinking of throwing an anti-boredom party at my place."

"Who's coming?" she asks.

"So far it's just me. Addie doesn't get back from her grandparents until tomorrow."

"Would you have room at your party for one more?"

"I think I can squeeze you in."

"I need to warn you, though," she adds. "When I get bored, I tend to get really affectionate. Will that be a problem?"

"Nothing I can't handle. I'm used to women throwing themselves at me."

She laughs and we sign off a few moments later. I am suddenly very keen to get home.

Our plane lands at San Jose at 2:50 and I'm home by 3:30. After dumping my bag in the apartment, I go downstairs to the office.

"The great white hunter has returned," observes Quinn.

"How have things been back here?" I ask.

"Surprisingly busy. I've taken calls from two new insurance companies, looking for a regular investigator. I took a case on for one of them, and I've finished it already; a workers' compensation claim."

"You've already finished it?" I'm astonished.

"Yep. Took some photos of a guy playing golf who is supposed to have a badly injured wrist. I've written up the report and drafted an invoice. It's just waiting for your approval."

"Brilliant!"

"Plus, we had two walk-ins late yesterday afternoon. A missing person and a suspected cheating spouse. I've started files for both of them."

"Great! Things are looking up. Sounds like you don't need me around here at all."

"How did it go down south?"

I spend some time filling her in on what we discovered.

"So, what's next?" she asks.

"In terms of Cory's case, we've done all we can. There's nothing more that can be learned. Cory will just have to live with what he's discovered and accept what remains a mystery. I'll close off the file and send him a final invoice."

"I'm sensing there's a 'but'."

"Yes. I think I have a moral obligation to pass on what we've discovered to the FBI. There's clearly a well-organized child-trafficking operation on our side of the border that needs investigating. I'm planning on contacting the FBI field office in San Francisco tomorrow."

Quinn finishes up soon after and heads off on her bike to catch up with some friends. I'm just about to lock up for the afternoon when I receive an unexpected visitor.

Senior Detective Elijah Abrams shuffles through the door, looking as crumpled and worn as ever.

"Detective Abrams. What can I do for you?"

"I was just passing. Thought I'd pop in for a chat," he says, plonking himself down in a chair opposite my desk. I'm trying to work out if the brown stain on the left breast of his cardigan is fresh or old. I think it's fresh.

He looks around, taking everything in.

"I see you haven't patched up the bullet holes yet."

"I thought they were some kind of brick borer until your College work-experience forensic guy told me they were bullet holes. It's amazing what these forensic guys can work out just from looking at stuff."

Abrams ignores my comment and decides to get straight to the point.

"I've seen some disturbing CCTV footage. There was a fight in a parking lot at a bowling alley last Thursday night. You wouldn't happen to know anything about that, would you?"

"That's five days ago, Detective. I have a terrible memory."

"Do you do much bowling?"

"Not a lot. I'm more of a croquet and champagne kind of guy."

"Funny thing is," he continues, ignoring my flippancy, "one of the guys in the fight looks a lot like you. In fact, he looks exactly like you. Same face, same build, same everything."

"What a coincidence. I must have a doppelganger out there somewhere."

"Amazing coincidence," he agrees, fixing me with a steady gaze. "We received a complaint about a fight in the parking lot, from a concerned member of the public. A bloke taking his wife and kids out for a night of fun at the local bowling alley."

He just looks at me and I stare right back at him.

"We checked the bowling alley's security camera footage. Turns out the guy who looks like you was acting in self-defense. My partner would love to bring charges against everyone involved, but the two thugs who started the fight seem to have disappeared."

"How is dear old Rosario these days? Such a gentle, caring soul."

Abrams gives me a piercing look, then says, "I'm going to have to ask you to come down to the station."

My heartrate immediately increases. I thought I'd been careful enough to ensure that I couldn't possibly be charged.

"Why? What have I done? What's the charge?"

"No charge. At least I hope there'll be no charge. But if you want to charge a moderate fee, we could probably negotiate something."

Now I'm confused.

"Err ... do you want to tell me what the hell we're talking about here?"

"The thing is, Doc, our boys and girls in blue are out there every day, putting their lives on the line. Most of them are good people who believe in what they're doing and are committed to keeping the public safe from bad guys. But it's a dangerous job and sometimes things get rough. The self-defense training that our academy gives them is very basic and, for officers who graduated years ago, they've probably forgotten much of what they were taught back then anyway. Every year we lose good cops because they aren't adequately trained to deal with hand to hand engagement."

"And you'd like me to run some classes?"

"Well, I was hoping to get the guy in the CCTV footage, but seeing we can't find him, you'll have to do."

He smiles at me now. It does something weird to his face, as if his muscles aren't used to doing it. I think I like him better when he's scowling.

"What did you have in mind?"

"I've talked it over with the boss. We thought we might start with a monthly class. Make it compulsory for a different group of officers each month – include it in their duty roster. The aim would be that every officer has at least two classes every year."

He pauses and looks at me. "Interested?"

"Yes. Definitely. I'd like to help."

"Good. We'll work on some dates and times and get back to you."

He stands and starts to walk toward the door, then stops and turns back to me.

"Oh. One more thing. That bad guy you hammered at the 7-Eleven last week was arraigned for first degree murder today. The judge denied bail and sent him to a maximum-security prison while he awaits trial. Looks like he's not coming back out for a very long time."

"One less scumbag on the streets," I say.

"Amen. But you might want to be a bit careful for the next few days. His gang aren't going to be very happy about this latest development. I wouldn't go wandering around late at night if I was you."

"Thanks for the tip, but I think I'll be OK."

I hope I sound more confident than I feel.

28

Claire arrives a bit after 6:00. I open the door and she's standing there looking stunning. Tight black jeans, boots and a tight-fitting cream top with a plunging neckline. Nothing fancy about the clothes; it's what's in them that is breath-taking. What is meant to be a quick kiss 'hello' lasts considerably longer, but eventually we come up for air.

"Are you going to ask me in, or will we keep making out in the doorway?"

"I don't mind where we make out."

She smiles and walks in, looking around.

"It's not much," I say, apologetically. "And it definitely lacks a feminine touch. But it does Addie and I just fine."

She deposits a bottle of wine in the fridge and I show her around. It takes all of three seconds, because there isn't much to see. I take her down to the office and she raises her eyebrows when she sees the horrible, threadbare carpet and the green and orange striped curtain that covers the opening to the rear hall.

"What kind of style were you trying for down here?"

"I was going for the up-market luxurious condo look."

"I hate to break it to you, but you didn't quite get there."

We end up back in the apartment and I start putting our dinner on the table while she pours us some wine. I bought a large antipasto platter from a very funky deli a few blocks away. It includes a wide selection of delicious food: cold meats, cheeses, olives and other delicacies.

We eat at the dining table, sitting close together, sipping our wine, picking at the food platter, talking and laughing. There is no awkwardness at all. It just feels right. She makes a few comments indicating that she knows what happened to Jessie. It's obvious that Billie has filled her in.

"It must have been devastating for you both," she says.

"Yes. Ripped our world apart. But we're doing OK now, I think."

"More than OK, I'd say," she observes. "Addie seems an incredibly well-adjusted girl. That says a lot about you as a single parent."

We take another sip of wine.

"What about you?" I ask. "Did you ever want children?"

"I definitely wanted children," she admits. "But I've never been with the right person at the right time. My engagement in my late twenties ended when my fiancé cheated on me. Then I finally did marry, here in California. We'd been married for three years and were about to start trying for children when I found out about an affair my husband had been having for years, even before he met me. That was two years ago. I'm thirty-seven now, and I think I may have missed my chance."

"It's still biologically possible, surely?"

"Possible, yes. But finding the right person is the difficult bit. I'm not prepared to bring a child into the world unless I can provide a secure home with two loving parents."

There is silence between us for the first time tonight, as her words hang in the air.

She turns to me, suddenly serious. "Look, John. It's probably good that you raised the issue, because I don't want to mislead you. I'm not looking for a casual fling. I'm beyond that. I'm looking for a forever partner; someone to share my life with and grow old with and, hopefully, make a baby with. If that's not you, if it's not what you're looking for, then it's better that we end this now and don't waste each other's time."

I nod and take a moment to gather my thoughts.

"Claire, I'm not looking for a casual fling either. As a matter of fact, I've never had one. I've only ever had one sexual partner in my whole life, and that was my wife, Jessie. I'm looking for exactly the same thing as you." I pause, not quite knowing how to word this. "Addie and I are a family. But lately, I've realized that ... I don't know how to express it ... we aren't a home. There's something missing; something I can't give her. And I don't want to scare you away, because we've only seen each other a few times and I know it's still early in our relationship, but these last few days with you have felt like ... home."

"What about the idea of having a baby?"

"I have to be honest and say that I haven't really thought about having another baby. But the idea doesn't frighten me at all. If it was with ... someone like you ... I think it would be wonderful."

She looks at me now, her eyes intent, and says, "John Targett, where have you been hiding all my life?" She kisses me tenderly, and somehow it holds the promise of a new beginning for both of us.

After clearing away our plates we take our wine to the lounge, and sit cuddling together, talking and listening to what Addie would call "old timers' music". Eventually we end up in each other's arms and she draws me down to lie with her on the lounge. I am lost in the softness of her mouth and I feel her responding to me with her whole body. I'm not sure how long we kiss for but we reach a point where it becomes obvious to both of us that we either stop now or go the whole way. By some kind of unspoken mutual consent, we pull back from the brink. Neither of us are prudes, but I sense that we want our first time to mean something more than a make-out session on a tired old lounge. We end up lying together in each other's arms and talking.

I open my eyes some time later and the apartment is completely dark. I sit up and find that there is a blanket over me. I switch on the nearby lamp and see a note on the coffee table.

"Thanks for a lovely night. I didn't want to wake you. XXX."

I look at my watch. 2:15 am. I stand up and stretch, then walk to the kitchen. Leaving the light off, I grab a glass from the cupboard and have a drink of water.

And that's when I nearly die.

As I reach down to get a dish towel from a drawer, a bullet smashes through the window and plows into the ceiling. I hit the ground as a second bullet smashes through the kitchen window. I hear a further two gunshots and then a car engine roars and wheels squeal, as a car races off down the rear laneway, its sound quickly fading into the distance.

Almost immediately I hear the sound of smashing glass from downstairs, then two more gunshots, followed by a car taking off along the main road. I run into my bedroom and get my Glock 19 and cautiously descend the stairs. Quinn told me earlier that she wouldn't be back tonight, so I know that if there is someone downstairs, it's not her.

There's no one there. I check everything carefully. The front window has been smashed again, and on the carpet, I find another brick – this time with the igloo symbol of the Eskimos painted on it, in still-wet yellow paint. There are two fresh bullet holes in the wall that adjoins the kitchen.

Detective Abrams was right. The Eskimos have hit back in anger over today's arraignment of their gang member.

I go back upstairs to check Addie's bedroom, and what I

find shocks me to the core. Addie's bedroom has a floor to ceiling window that faces the rear lane. Two bullets have shattered the window, low down, and have passed diagonally through her mattress, entering at the side and exiting through the top of the mattress where Addie would normally be lying. My beautiful daughter would now be dead if she had been home tonight. I feel sick in the stomach and I sit on the edge of her bed, shaking. It's clear to me now, that this gang isn't going to stop. They have me firmly in their sights and, because of that, Addie's life is now in grave danger.

As I sit with my gun in my hand, a rising tide of anger consumes me. This is my home. This is where my daughter lives. How dare they! Then my anger turns from rage to something darker and colder. They've crossed a line, and they are going to regret it.

Because I've decided it's time to go to war.

29

———

It takes nearly an hour to clean up the broken glass, after which I drag an inflatable air mattress downstairs and get some light sleep while keeping guard over the compromised office. Costa pays me a visit with a freshly brewed black coffee at 6:15, having seen the broken window and guessed that I might need some encouragement. It turns out the gang threw a brick through the Beanstalk window too, so they must have worked out that I own both shops.

"Mr. John. What will you do about this? You gonna call the cops?"

"I probably will, but it won't do much good."

"So, what will you do?"

"I'm going to put a stop to it."

"How?"

"Don't worry. I'm going to work something out."

"You be careful, Mr. John. Don't do anything stupid, hey? These people are dangerous."

"Yes. But they're also incredibly dumb. That means I've got the advantage. Don't worry, Costa, I'll fix this."

"If you need help, you call me, yes? I did national service. I can handle a gun."

"Thanks Costa, but I think I'll manage."

By 8:00 I've spoken to the glazier and the police. At 8:15, Quinn comes through the back door and sees the damage.

"Holy crap!"

"You can say that again."

"Holy crap!"

"Very funny."

"When did this happen?"

"Around 2:15."

I tell Quinn about the shots fired into the apartment upstairs, as well.

"Were they aimed at you, specifically?"

"I think so. I was standing at the sink at the time. If I hadn't bent down when I did, I wouldn't be here now."

"But why now, after more than a week of silence?"

"I'm pretty sure it's a reprisal as a result of the gang member's arraignment yesterday."

"So do you think that's the end of it now?"

"No. It's not going to stop. I can see that now. There's a trial to come, and a conviction, and probably some failed appeals into the future. No, these guys are going to keep coming after me, and every fresh step along the legal pathway is going to stir up renewed anger."

"So, what are you going to do?"

"I'm going to take the battle to them. I'm going to make them regret that they started this."

Quinn looks at me intently. I'm beyond angry now. I'm in full battle mode and I'm already planning and calculating my moves. I move to my desk, speaking to her as I do.

"I want you to see if you can track the two cars from last night. See if you can find where they came from and where they went. Also, I want to know whether our Eskimo pal, Antonio Sanchez is sticking to his regular, evening routine."

"Roger. I'm on it."

We spend the morning engrossed in our online tasks. A little after ten, the police arrive and, after careful examination of all the evidence, are able to confirm that someone shot up my home and office again. I can see that our tax-payer dollars are being put to good use.

Around lunchtime, I give Claire a call. She's working day shift and I manage to catch her on her lunch break.

"Hello, sleepy head," she says.

"Sorry about that."

"No need to apologize. I really enjoyed last night."

"So did I."

"At least I discovered one extremely important fact about you," she says.

"Which is?"

"You don't snore."

"Would that have been a deal breaker?"

"Maybe. I'm a very fussy girl."

We chat for a while longer and I explain that I'll be working some odd hours for the rest of the week, particularly at night. We decide to do a replay of last Saturday's soccer date, by which time I think I will have finished the 'special case' I'm working on.

By early afternoon Quinn has some results. She followed the CCTV trace for the car out the front for several miles before losing it. She had more luck with the car in the lane out the back. It turns out to have been the same car from the previous attack. It was returned to the same location and Quinn was able to identify Sanchez's car leaving that area shortly after. He returned to the same industrial area for a brief time before returning home at around 4:00 am.

"It looks like Sanchez is a creature of habit," says Quinn.

"Yes. It also looks as though that industrial area is definitely some kind of gang headquarters."

"So, what's next?" she asks.

"Surveillance. I'm going to follow Sanchez's car tonight and find where he goes."

"Can I come?"

"No. I'd prefer that you didn't. I know I said I'd teach you surveillance, but this is dangerous."

"Are you going to be safe?"

"Yes."

"Good. I'm coming with you."

"I just told you, it's dangerous."

"No, you just told me you'll be safe. I'm coming."

"I'm not taking you."

"We'll see."

I shake my head and give up for the moment. I have to make a phone call. Karl answers after a couple of rings.

"Hey dude, what's happening?"

"Karl, I need to ask a big favor."

"Shoot."

"Jessie's parents have been looking after Addie while I've been gone. They're picking her up from school and dropping her home along with all her stuff this afternoon."

"Uh huh."

"The thing is, buddy, it's not safe for her here at the moment."

"Has something else happened?"

"They shot the place up again last night. Nearly put a bullet through my head at the kitchen window."

"Shit!"

"Yeah. Anyway, I don't want to ask Mort and Katherine to mind her again, because they'll start to get wind that something isn't right. They already think I'm a bad influence and I don't want to give them an excuse to try to take her from me again."

"Yeah, yeah, John. I get it. You don't have to even ask, buddy. You know we love Addie like she was our own. There's a bed here for her as long as you need."

"Thanks, Karl."

"So what are you going to do, dude? You can't let this keep happening."

"I'm not going to. I'm gonna make it stop."

"How?"

"I'm still working on that. But, for the moment, I just need to know Addie is safe."

"Sure. We'll come over and pick her up around 5:00 if that helps."

"Thanks."

By 4:00 pm, the glazier has replaced all the broken windows and I've spent a few more hours in research. I'm starting to formulate a plan but it won't work unless I can accurately identify where Sanchez is going every night.

Addie comes bustling in the door soon after 4:00 and gives me a kiss on the cheek.

"Hi Dad! Did you miss me?"

"No, not at all. It was peaceful and quiet."

"Ha ha. Very funny."

"Of course I missed you," I say, giving her a hug and feeling emotional all of a sudden. This is my little girl – the girl whose life I will do anything to protect.

Mort and Katherine come through the door as we are hugging. They are carrying Addie's gear between them. We have some small talk and I offer them a cup of tea or coffee but they decline. I thank them once again for looking after Addie and for their generous gift of the car. It's still awkward between us, and they don't stay long, but it's a start.

Once they've left, I sit down with Addie and explain that I am going to be working some very odd hours for the next few days and I need her to stay with Billie and Karl. She tries to convince me that she can stay here and look after herself if I'm not around, but I am adamant and she soon realizes that I won't be swayed.

Shortly before 5:00, Karl and Billie arrive to pick Addie up. While Billie helps Addie finish packing, Karl takes me aside. He's got an overnight bag with him.

"Dude, I don't know what you're planning to do, but I'm staying here with you until we see this thing through."

"This isn't your fight, Karl."

"Of course it is! You and Addie are family. No way I'm going to let you go off and do some damn fool thing on your own. I'm here to make sure you don't get yourself into too much trouble."

"You don't have to worry about me; I'm not going to do anything too stupid. But I'm gonna make this right."

"Good!" says Karl. "And I'm gonna to be there with you to make sure you don't get your ass shot off in the process."

"What have you got in the bag?" I ask him.

"Toothpaste, pajamas and guns. Just the basic essentials."

"We won't be needing any guns tonight. This is just basic surveillance."

"So what's your big plan?"

"I'll tell you tomorrow if tonight goes the way I hope it does."

30

—————

By 5:30 pm Karl and I are in place. We're sitting in my car a couple of hundred yards past the last CCTV camera on De La Cruz Boulevard, where we always lose contact with Antonio Sanchez's car. Quinn was very keen to accompany us, but I gave her an important job to do back at the office. She's now watching a live stream from the CCTV camera closest to Sanchez's home. She'll phone me as soon as she sees him drive past the camera and she'll keep updating us as he passes each successive one. Most nights, Sanchez seems to leave home around 6:00, so we shouldn't have long to wait.

"I see you've brought your best pal along with you," I say, indicating the bulge in Karl's jacket pocket.

"Just to keep us company," he says, patting his pocket.

"Sig Sauer P320?"

"Of course. Best handgun in the world."

We've had this argument before. Several times. He knows I'm a Glock man and won't be swayed.

"Glock's lighter," I say.

"Sig packs two more rounds," he counters.

"Glock's barrel lasts four times longer,"

"Sig looks like a real gun, not a toy."

"Glock's easier to conceal."

"Sig can be modified for different calibers."

We're silent for a moment.

"Thanks for being here, Karl."

"You haven't got my invoice yet."

It's 6:05 when we get the call from Quinn.

"He's on his way."

I start the engine. Quinn talks to me as Sanchez passes the next three CCTV cameras and by now it's clear he's following his usual route.

"He's just passed the last camera now. You should be able to see his headlights."

"Yep. Got him in my rear vision mirror. Thanks Quinn."

We let him drive past. It's the same dark blue Chevy Suburban we've tracked in the CCTV cameras . There's a second car about fifty yards behind him so I wait for it to pass as well and then pull out behind it. Sanchez turns second left. I pull over at the corner and watch him drive the length of the short street. As he turns right at the T junction at the far end I turn into the street and put my foot down. At the far intersection, we look to the right and see Sanchez turn into a parking area at the front of a small factory unit, about a hundred yards up the road. As we watch, he gets out of his car and walks into the unit. It's hard to make out any details, because the unit is in a dark pocket of the street, with the nearest streetlights eighty yards on either side of it.

We park at a safe distance, on the opposite side of the road to the shed, which gives me a better angle of view. I switch off the engine and crack the windows to avoid fogging up. There is another car already in the small parking lot in the front of the factory unit and over the next hour three motorcycles and five other vehicles arrive. The last is another Chevy suburban;

black this time. It's driven by a guy wearing sunglasses even though it's night. Four scantily-clad women in high heels and mini-skirts get out of the vehicle and enter the unit.

"And for tonight's entertainment," says Karl, "we have Betty, Bessy, Beckie and Bonnie, the Bimbo sisters."

About an hour later, the girls re-emerge and leave with the same driver.

"I'd say they just gave their bosses a freebie before starting work for the night," Karl comments.

Around 10:30 a guy emerges from the front door of the shed, starts his motorcycle and rides down what seems to be a side driveway, out of sight from our position. After ten minutes I decide to go for a walk past the shed to see what's happening.

"Are sure that's a good idea?" says Karl.

"I'll be OK. I'll stick to the sidewalk on this side."

"Just be careful, dude."

I get out of the car and walk along the shadowed sidewalk, my hands in my jacket pockets and my zipper closed to the top in the brisk, late-February night air. The gang's base is a small steel-clad unit, about thirty feet wide and sixty feet deep. At the front there is a large glass sliding door in the middle with a glass window on either side. Their unit is flanked by much larger brick buildings, housing rows of factory bays with large steel roller-doors. As I walk past the gang's shed, I see the driveway which goes down the side, providing access to a side roller-door toward the rear. The roller door is fully open and light is spilling out from inside. The motorcycle is parked in the open bay and two guys are working on it with tools in one hand and beer bottles in the other. Work benches littered with tools line the sides of the bay, and there are several car jacks and car tires on display.

I turn and walk back toward our car. There is loud hip-hop music coming from inside the shed, and muted light spills out from the curtained windows and doors. There is a narrow concrete path running down the other side of the shed providing access to several air conditioning units and propane gas bottles.

Back in my car, I tell Karl what I saw in the bay.

"No drug lab equipment?" he asks.

"No, and I didn't expect there to be any. They may be stupid but they're not so dumb as to crap in their own backyard. If they do run a drug lab it won't be at their clubhouse. It's likely to be in some run-down house in a quiet corner of suburbia."

"So what's going on here, then?"

"I'd say the shed used to be operated as an auto repair business. I think they just use the rear work bay to tinker with their own vehicles now."

Karl and I settle down to watch. Surveillance is a boring business and I eventually tell Karl to put his seat back and get some sleep, promising to wake him if I need him. After another hour with no further car arrivals, I decide to get some shut-eye as well. I set my watch timer for an hour and close my eyes. Karl is lightly snoring beside me; he'd never make a good surveillance operative. I've developed the ability to doze lightly while still being aware of my surroundings.

My watch pings me every hour throughout the night and I spend five minutes checking the environment, looking for car movements and any major changes. At around 2:00 am I decide to do another walk past. I wake Karl and let him know.

"Dude, you be careful, OK?"

"Sure. I just need another quick look."

I retrace my steps from earlier. This time I'm particularly interested in the path down the nearest side of the building. I stand across the road directly opposite the path, looking carefully and calculating. I'm back in the car five minutes later, having seen everything I need.

"So, what's the plan, dude?" asks Karl when I get back.

"I'm still working on it. Get some more sleep. I'm staying till the end."

Around 3:00, cars start leaving, one by one. By 4:00 they are all gone and we do a slow drive-by. The lights are off and the place is deserted. I turn around and drive home through deserted streets, with a plan slowly crystalizing in my mind.

31

———

At 8:00 am the next morning, I drop Karl at his gun shop then head back out to the gang's headquarters. I don't expect to see anyone there and I'm right. I do a drive by. The steel shed with its empty parking lot is sleeping peacefully in the midst of a now bustling industrial area. Cars and vans are coming and going, the street is packed with parked cars, and various industrial sounds can be heard emanating from the open factory bays. I park and do another walk past, then spend another two incredibly boring hours sitting in the car and eventually return home with my suspicions confirmed and my plan now much clearer.

Back at the office Quinn asks me how it went and I describe to her the long, tedious hours of surveillance. She really didn't miss much.

"So what do you want me to do today?" she asks.

"Firstly, I want you to write up a full report on everything we've discovered in the Cory Wainwright case. Dates, payments, birth certificate discrepancies, the conflicting photos, the conflicting baby health record books, details of the deleted hospital file, the laboratory diagnosis, and the corporate links between the various companies associated with Acorn Adoption Agency, including their ownership of the orphanage in Monterrey."

"What's the report for?"

"I'm planning to hand it over to the FBI."

"There's only one problem with that," she replies. "I discovered the deleted hospital file and the laboratory diagnosis by, shall we say, questionable electronic means."

"I understand your concern, but I'm not about to implicate you in any way. All we need to say is that we became aware of certain facts. We won't say how. The FBI can check those facts for themselves and when they do, they will be much more concerned with prosecuting the bad guys than twisting our arms to find out how we came across the information."

"OK. As long as you're sure we won't get slapped in irons and sent to the gulag."

"No gulag, I promise. Once, you've finished the report, I'll add my findings from my trip to Mexico, including an attached link to the recording of my conversation with Mamá Rosa. By the time we've finished, the whole package will be enough to make even the most hardened FBI agent salivate."

As Quinn starts work on the report, I make a few phone calls. I need to hire a delivery van. Once I've organized that for Friday morning, I ring a couple of companies that supply large oxygen bottles to hospitals and heavy industry. I negotiate a price for two large, fully-charged bottles which they promise to deliver this afternoon. I then drive to a hardware store and buy two cans of yellow spray paint, some white overalls, leather riggers gloves, a decent wrench, a large red trolley, a gas hose with a splitter and two couplings, a couple of U-shaped fixing clips and some self-tapping screws. The next stop is a second-hand clothing store where I buy a plain white baseball cap, slightly marked. Finally, I head to a local mall where I know there is a store that does same-day embroidery. I leave them my cap and overalls and spend an hour wandering around aimlessly. I find a café and order a tuna and salad sandwich. Quinn would be proud of me. Eventually, I pick up my cap and overalls and head back to the office, dumping everything on the floor beside my desk.

Quinn is still working on the report, so I leave her to it. There is one more item that I will need, and only Karl can help me with that. His gun shop is located in a light industrial area in Sunnyvale. It's a concrete block building with its own parking lot. The shop is located at the front of the building and the back is dedicated to an impressive shooting range. A huge sign dominates the wall above the large glass entrance to the building, saying, "Destrier Guns and Shooting Range". It's a thriving business and Karl and Billie are not short of a dollar.

Walking through the door, I am greeted by rows and rows of every gun imaginable. It's a gun enthusiast's paradise. The four staff on duty are wearing black polo shirts with "Destrier Guns" embroidered in bright yellow, and there are at least six customers browsing the merchandise.

Karl spots me immediately and comes over to greet me.

"How are you feeling?" I ask him.

"A bit tired," he admits. "I don't handle the late nights like I used to."

"I know what you mean," I sympathize.

"What brings you here? Are you up for a shoot?"

"Yeah. I am. I'm also looking for a new bit of gear. I need a gun that's extremely quiet."

"You know that silencers are illegal in California, don't you?" Karl asks.

"Yes, I do. Is there any other option?"

"There are some guns that are specifically designed to be quiet. How quiet do you need it to be?"

"Very."

He nods thoughtfully and then says, "Come with me."

We go into his back office and he fiddles with the combination of a large safe, bigger than two refrigerators combined. He swings the door open and I see several shelves of weapons and other items. He takes a gun out and hands it to me.

"This is the mother of all quiet weapons, dude."

I look at it curiously. It looks like either a very long pistol or a very short carbine. The entire thing is metal, no wood or plastic anywhere.

"What is it?"

"It's a replica of a bolt-action 1945 De Lisle Carbine. It has a modified Thompson submachine gun barrel and uses .45 ACP subsonic rounds. This is the model with the folding metal stock." He demonstrates by folding it out, transforming the gun into a small carbine, then folding it back in again.

"And it's quiet?"

"One of the quietest guns ever made."

"I'll take it."

"I can't sell it to you, dude. But I'll lend it to you."

"Is it legal?"

"Borderline. I wouldn't want to get caught with it in my possession." He gives me a discerning look. "When do you need it, and what are you using it for?"

"I'd like to borrow it for tomorrow night. I want to shoot some holes in some car doors."

"You won't be pointing it at people?"

"Nope. Never shot anyone in my life and don't intend to start now if I can help it."

"OK. How about we go down to the shooting range and get you familiar with it?"

We spend the next two hours at the range while his staff manage the store. Just as he said, the De Lisle is quiet but it's still going to make a bit of a bang. It takes about ten minutes to calibrate it and get used to its action. After that, Karl and I then spend the rest of the time firing several varieties of guns that he has on-hand as demos. I can't come close to Karl's level of marksmanship, but I don't disgrace myself either. By the end of the two hours I've regained most of the proficiency that I've lost since leaving the army.

As I leave with the De Lisle safely tucked away in a gun bag, Karl asks what time tomorrow night we'll be heading out.

"You're not coming," I say. "This is a solo operation now."

"Like hell it is! There's no way I'm letting you go into danger alone."

"I'll be fine. I'm not planning on running into any bad guys."

"No one ever plans to run into bad guys, dude. But shit happens. This is not negotiable. If you don't let me come with you; I take the gun back. Simple as that."

I sigh. It's not ideal, but I can see that I don't have a choice. "OK."

We arrange a time and I head home. I'm planning an early night to catch up on sleep, because tomorrow night things might get a bit hectic.

32

I wake on Thursday morning after a good night's sleep, feeling fully recharged. After an early morning run, I unfold the martial arts training tower from the corner of the office where it's now being stored. I go through a forty-minute routine and try to be as quiet as possible, but I was being extremely optimistic in thinking that it wouldn't wake Quinn. I see her head poking through the striped curtain toward the end of the routine and I'm expecting a sarcastic remark about me waking her up, but she surprises me.

"Can you teach me that?"

"Really?"

"Yeah. I'd like to be able to kick the shit out of anyone who tries to mess with me."

"I'm going to start my next Women's Self-Defense Class on Tuesday night at the YMCA. Why don't you come along? It's free."

"I might. But can you teach me something now?"

A few minutes later she's changed out of her PJs and is dressed in shorts, T shirt and joggers. I spend thirty minutes showing her some basic moves and I'm surprised how quickly she picks it up. I'm doubly surprised by her strength and aggression. It appears that whatever Quinn does, she does it with one hundred percent commitment.

After we've both showered and changed, we walk into the Beanstalk and grab coffees.

"Mr. John! And Miss Quinn! Lovely to see you! What can I get you today?"

"I'll have a mocha decaf with almond milk."

"But you only drink ..." begins Quinn.

"Shhh!" I say.

"And for you Miss Quinn?"

I lean over and whisper, "Make up something ridiculous."

She gives me a strange look, then shrugs.

"Umm ... I'll have a cappuccino on rice milk with three sugars."

"Sure! Coming right up!"

A couple of minutes later he hands me my long black and Quinn gets her regular soy flat white with no sugar.

"How is it today, Mr. John?"

"Best you've ever made, Costa."

"I knew it! I'll put it on your tab."

As we walk out, Quinn shakes her head and asks, "What was that all about?"

"It's a daily ritual between friends. A private joke, if you like. It's a way of sharing a familiar moment."

She shakes her head. "Sometimes, I don't get men at all."

Back at the office I go over the new cases with her and give her a workers' compensation surveillance case to go on with. As she starts to do some research on the surveillance subject, I go over the report she produced on the baby swapping operation. After reading through the report and making a few amendments I spend another hour writing up my report of the Mexico trip. When I'm finally satisfied, I decide that it's time to contact the FBI field office in San Francisco.

I dial the phone number that I find on the internet and the agent I initially speak with suggests that I contact the satellite office, or 'resident agency' as she calls it, in San Jose. I don't think that's going to be good enough though, and I insist that I speak with someone who is able to deal with a serious ongoing felony that has international implications. Finally, I'm put through to Senior Special Agent Frank Morrison. I introduce myself and give him a run-down of my discoveries. He is interested but wary. I guess they must get a lot of calls from total nut cases. He gives me an email address to send my file to and says they'll get back to me if they have any further questions.

"Duty done!" I say as I send the email a few minutes later. "I've sent them the file. Now it's over to them."

"How did the agent seem?" asks Quinn.

"Guarded. Not totally convinced. But it's out of our hands now, and I have a clear conscience that we've done the right thing."

Quinn heads out of the office a few minutes later, after I give her a few pointers about basic surveillance techniques. Then I pick up my phone and text Claire.

Miss you. What time is lunch?

I get an immediate reply.

Soon. Maybe twenty minutes.

Want some company?

Yes, please.

I lock up the office and head to the hospital. Twenty minutes later, I'm sitting in the ED waiting room texting Claire that I'm here. A few minutes later the door to the consulting area opens and Claire sticks her head out.

"John Targett, please."

I smile and walk into the consulting area with her. She indicates for me to follow her and she takes me into one of the consulting bays and closes the curtain behind us.

"What seems to be the problem today, Mr. Targett?" she

asks quietly, with mock severity.

"I seem to have a bad case of love sickness."

"Love sickness? Really? Describe the symptoms"

"Shortness of breath, increased pulse rate and feelings of extreme euphoria whenever I am around a certain person."

"How long has this been going on?"

"Since the first time I laid eyes on her, actually, but it's been getting progressively worse."

"Oh dear. That sounds serious," she says trying to keep from smiling.

"Actually, I think it might be turning into something quite serious," I say. "Is there a cure?"

"Unfortunately, once it's progressed to this stage, there is no cure. All we can do now is alleviate the symptoms."

"What will that involve? Will it hurt?"

"Not at all. In fact, I think you'll find it quite pleasurable." She puts her arms around me and whispers, "This won't hurt a bit." She kisses me then, and I hold her close against me.

A few moments later a nurse pokes her head through the curtain and says with a cheeky smile, "When you two are finished playing doctors and nurses in here, I've got a patient who needs the bed." She gives me an appraising look, and then says to Claire, "I thought you said he was plain and boring? He looks kinda dishy to me."

Claire just smiles and shakes her head.

"John, this is Georgina. Don't believe anything she says."

Five minutes later we are sitting on a low brick wall in the sunshine, eating sandwiches from the cafeteria. She only has thirty minutes for lunch, and we spend it talking about nothing in particular, just enjoying being together. I don't want it to end, but all too soon she has to go back. We kiss briefly and I head back to my car. I wish the rest of my day was going to be that enjoyable, but I know it won't be. I've got some serious business to take care of tonight.

33

———

I have dinner at Karl and Billie's. It's good to spend time with Addie, as I haven't seen very much of her over the last few days. She is her usual self – intelligent, witty, flippant, cute, adorable, sarcastic and frustrating, all rolled into one. I love her to bits, and just seeing her again tonight makes me realize how important it is that I fix this situation, completely and permanently. I have to keep her safe.

Karl and I leave a little after 9:00, with Billie demanding that we don't do anything illegal or unsafe. I lie and say that I would never dream of it. Once we get to my apartment, I describe my plan to Karl.

"What do you think?" I ask, when I've finished explaining.

"It's got a lot of moving parts, dude. A lot of variables that could go horribly wrong."

"I'm aware of that. But have you got any better ideas?"

"Nope."

Karl crashes on the couch and we both manage to get a couple of hours sleep. At midnight we are awake and checking our gear. My contribution is two cans of yellow spray paint, a small step ladder and my own Glock 19 which I plan to keep in my pocket and not touch. Karl has got his Sig Sauer in his pocket, plus he's supplied the De Lisle Carbine with two fully loaded magazines, two black balaclavas and two Bedlam 860s which are folding tactical combat knives with a scimitar curve and an extremely sharp point. It pays to have a best friend who owns a weapons store.

We take my car because of its dark color and tinted windows. By 12:30 we're rolling, heading East, directly away from the Eskimo's headquarters. We're not going anywhere near it tonight. Our target is a church, in a mixed business and light industrial area north of San Jose, on the other side of the airport from Santa Clara. During the afternoon I got Quinn to check the locations of all the CCTVs in that immediate area and map out the best route to take in and out of the target. I've memorized the route and we arrive in the street a little after 1:00 am. I do a drive-by of the church, paying particular attention to the cars in the parking lot. The building is painted white and is a wooden construction in the classic design, with a steep-pitched slate roof and a bell tower and steeple at the front over the entrance foyer. A driveway goes down the right side and around the back, giving access to the designated car spaces that butt into the side and back perimeter fences.

We can't see all the car spaces around the back, but it looks like there could be about twelve cars and six motorcycles in the parking lot tonight. Light is shining from a series of tall, narrow stained-glass windows, and as I wind my own window down, I can hear reggae music blasting from inside, so loud that I imagine the foundations must be rattling.

"I don't think we have to worry about making noise, dude," says Karl.

I've done my research. The church was once a Jesuit parish and is one of the oldest church buildings in San Jose. When it was built, it was on the edge of a suburban housing area, but over the years changes in council zoning have allowed factory units and light industry to gradually encroach. Today the church stands alone, surrounded by industrial units with not a house in sight. The church became financially unsustainable many years ago and the building was sold to a private counselling service, who operated out of it for over a decade, constructing internal partitions for counselling rooms and offices. Twelve years ago, it was purchased by a registered company called the Brethren of Righteousness, who have owned it ever since. Too late, the council discovered that the company is a front for a criminal gang, the Reverends.

The Reverends are a Latino gang whose criminal exploits make the Eskimos look like amateurs. Within a few years, the Reverends became the most feared gang in San Jose, quickly expanding their territory and destroying other, weaker gangs. They are multi-talented: assassinations, arson, drug production and distribution, prostitution and extortion are some of their better-known activities. The church, which is what the gang still calls their headquarters, has been raided by police on several occasions, but the Reverends have either been warned in advance or they are extremely cautious about crapping in their own backyard, because police have never found anything to close down their premises.

The council has also sought legal advice regarding the possibility of challenging their ownership of the building, but the Reverends have ensured that their legal right to ownership is watertight.

I continue driving past the church, take two quick rights and drive down the parallel street behind. The church spire can be clearly seen over the low-slung factory units in this back street and when I am level with it, I turn into a driveway between two rows of industrial units, reverse-parking against the fence at the back that is shared with the church parking lot. I switch off the engine and we get our gear ready; a knife each, a spray can each, and I am also carrying the De Lisle. It's an old six-foot wooden fence and the rails are on the church side, so it will be easy to climb back over, but we need the step ladder on this side.

We're both wearing black clothing and now we put on our balaclavas. I climb the small step ladder and stand with my head poking over the fence, scanning the parking lot for almost a minute. There is no movement. We quickly scale the fence and squat down in the shadows in the corner where the back and side fences meet. It will be a two-phase operation, starting with the quietest and ending with the loudest. Sticking to the fence line and keeping the cars between us and the church, we both begin scurrying along the line of cars and bikes, with Karl moving along the back fence and me crouching along the side fence toward the front.

As we come to each car or bike, we spray the Eskimo gang tag on the vehicle and then plunge a knife into two tires. Bikes have both tires blown. Cars lose the two closest to the fence. It takes a lot longer than I had anticipated, because some of the tires are steel belted radials and they take several plunges of the knife before they puncture. At least fifteen minutes have passed by the time Karl and I meet back at the corner. I had hoped we'd be gone by now and Karl is starting to get worried. The longer we stay, the more chance there is of someone coming out of the church and seeing us.

"Dude, let's just get out of here!" says Karl urgently. "We've done enough."

I fold my knife and put it in my pocket.

"You go and start the car," I tell him. "I'll be right behind you."

Before Karl can argue, I pick up the De Lisle and scurry along the fence line to the start of the parking lot near the street. My heart is beating like a jackhammer now, because this is the moment when I'm about to commit a serious crime. I'm also about to place myself in mortal danger. There are seriously dangerous dudes in that building and if they hear the gun and come out, I doubt I will make it over the back fence alive.

A seriously-loud reggae song is playing now, with a big snare beat, and I time my first shot to coincide with the snare. Bang! Straight through driver's door. The bullet would have ripped into the driver's seat as well, making a bit of a mess. I move to the next car. Bang! Right on the beat, through the driver's door again. One bullet per car. Move. Fire. Move. Fire. Every shot on the beat. I skip the motorcycles and just hit the cars. I'm not trying to disable the vehicles, just damage them and infuriate the owners. I get to the corner of the fence and change magazines, putting the used one into my jacket pocket, and snapping in a fresh one. Then I start along the line of cars at the back. Move. Fire. Move. Fire. Finally I've finished, but before I go, I've just thought of one last touch. I grab the can of spray paint from my jacket pocket and start painting a huge Eskimo tag across the entire tarmac of the back parking lot.

I've barely finished when a side door to the church opens, spilling light and sound from inside. Two bearded, heavily tattooed guys in leather walk out, talking loudly over the music. They close the door and start walking toward two motorcycles, parked side-by-side directly in front of them, mid-way along the side parking area. I'm in shadow at the back fence and I run to the corner and scale the fence like a cat. As I land, I hear cursing coming from the parking lot then the sound of yelling and boots running across the tarmac. I dive into the passenger side of the car.

"Go! Go! Go!"

Karl doesn't need any encouragement. We're out of the driveway like a rocket and he nearly turns right.

"No! No! Left! There's a camera to the right!"

My heart is practically beating out of my chest, and I'm soaked with nervous sweat. My hands are shaking now, in a nervous reaction, as we drive away from the scene of the crime.

And it was a crime. I am fully aware of that. I've never done anything like it before. I have always been a law-abiding citizen who decries needless violence and senseless arson. But even a law-abiding man will go to extreme lengths to safeguard his family.

"We did it, man! We did it!" exclaims Karl as I continue to guide him on our camera-free exit route. "Shit! I've never been so scared!"

"Me too, bro," I say. "I'd much rather fight someone hand to hand than do that."

"That's because you're a bloody lethal weapon. The rest of us poor sods have to run when we get threatened."

We make it safely out of the area, without any sign of pursuit. As I drop Karl back at his house at 2:50, we fist pump.

"Try to get some decent sleep, Karl, because tomorrow night is the grand finale."

"Will do, bro."

I get home and shower and try to sleep, but it won't come. The adrenaline is still coursing through my system, so I get up and spend forty minutes running up and down the stairs outside my office. Another shower and a double nip of whisky eventually do the job.

One operation down.

The biggest, yet to come.

34

My alarm wakes me at 8:00. I feel like warmed-up road-kill and I'd love to sleep longer, but I have important work to do this morning. I grab a quick coffee from Costa and drive to the car rental place that I phoned a couple of days ago.

They've got a new model Chevrolet Express 3500 Cargo Van ready for me. I sign the paperwork, leave my car in the street outside their lot and then head back to the office. Quinn is up by now and watches my preparations with interest as she sips her green concoction of swamp water. The oxygen bottles arrived late yesterday afternoon, so I load them into the van and strap them in. They are huge industrial sized bottles, much bigger than those used in hospital wards. Working efficiently and quickly, I load the rest of the gear into the van: step ladder, trolley and gas bottle hose. I pack my tool kit with the wrench, my old battery-operated driver, the self-tapping screws and the U-shaped fixing clips. I also chuck in a pair of pliers as well, as I think I might need them. I change into the overalls and cap and ask Quinn what she thinks.

"Gerry's Gas Bottle Service? You couldn't come up with a better name than Gerry?"

"I considered 'Tom and Gerry', but it wouldn't fit on the cap."

She's aware of my plan and asks if I'm sure I don't need help.

"No. These kind of tradesmen always work alone. I have to look authentic."

I head out in the van and reach the Eskimo's factory unit by 9:15. It's Friday morning and the whole street is humming. Numerous vans similar to mine and even bigger are making deliveries and picking up goods. I drive slowly past the metal shed and confirm that the parking lot is empty and the place is locked up, then I drive back and reverse directly into the car spot on the far left. There's a four-foot-wide concrete path running down the left side of the shed, giving access to a couple of air-conditioning units and a large propane gas bottle. But what interests me are the four small air vent grills at regular intervals down the side of the shed. I spotted them on my daytime drive by on Wednesday and that's when my plan began to crystalize.

I put my riggers' gloves on and unload the two large oxygen bottles, levering them off the back of the van. Using the trolley, I wheel them, one at a time, around the side and deposit them directly underneath the vent closest to the front of the shed. Once both bottles are in place, I grab my step-ladder and the rest of the gear and head back to the bottles. To anyone who might be watching, I would look like a legitimate gas bottle supplier delivering a couple of new bottles to a customer. I shuffle the bottles until they are hard up against the side of the shed, then I attach the hose with dual couplings to the bottles, tightening the fittings with the wrench.

The final step is the one that might look suspicious if anyone is watching. I glance around behind me. The side path is bordered by a thin grass strip with chest high shrubs. On the other side of that is a wide concrete driveway servicing the row of industrial units next door. All of the units have large roller shutter doors that are open, and inside most of the bays I can see workers welding, banging, sawing, drilling and sanding as they carry out their various tasks. No one is even remotely interested in me.

I climb up the stepladder and investigate the external grill of the air vent. It's a small, circular grill, made of flimsy white plastic. I put my face up to the grill and I can see an identical internal grill covered in fly mesh about three inches further in. Peering through that, I can see into the shed itself. It is a large open front room running the entire width of the shed, with an eclectic variety of battered old lounges and sofas scattered around the space. There is a pool table and a soccer table as well. Empty beer bottles and chip packets litter several small coffee tables and I identify a variety of drug paraphernalia lying around. Looking as far as I can to the right, I can just see the front right window. The room is perfect for what I intend.

I take my pliers from my back pocket and grab the lowest plastic vane in the external grill. Wiggling it up and down and twisting from side to side, I manage to snap a section of it away. I then stick the gas hose through the newly-opened hole in the air vent, pushing it in as far as it will go. Next I take one of the small U-shaped saddle clips and place it over the hose where it enters the vent. Using my cordless driver and a couple of self-tapping screws, I quickly screw the clip to the grill. Climbing back down, I swivel the gas bottles and adjust their position so the hose sits snuggly against the wall and isn't obvious from the street, then I attach the second saddle clip to the shed wall, holding the hose tightly in place.

Job done.

There's no way the oxygen bottles can be traced back to me. I purchased them under the name, 'The Brethren of Righteousness', and gave the church address as the place of business. I paid cash and presented the supplier with a fake O2 Compliance Certificate, produced with Quinn's expertise. Of course, if they ever do get traced back to me, I'll be in deep 'doo-doo', but with every additional law I break, I think of Addie, grit my teeth and push ahead. What else can a father do?

I make sure the valves on the oxygen bottles are turned off, then I pack up my gear. I take the trolley and tool kit back to the van and I'm just turning back to retrieve my step ladder when a voice shouts at me.

"Hey buddy!"

I turn and see a big guy in grease-stained blue overalls walking across the road toward me. I might have to ditch the step ladder and just get out of here.

"Are you the gas supplier?"

He's standing right in front of me now, staring at the embroidery on my cap and overalls. I'm not sure what he thinks 'Gerry's Gas Bottle Service' implies. Pizza delivery?

"Sure am," I reply.

"How much do you charge?"

I have to think quickly.

"How much are you paying at the moment?"

"Two fifty a quarter, plus one fifty for every exchange bottle."

"They're ripping you off, man."

"Don't I know it!"

"We can do a lot better than that. I don't have any brochures with me at the moment because it's a brand-new van, but I'm back in the area again on Monday. I'll drop a brochure in and we can talk dollars then."

"Sweet. I'm in the second unit down the driveway straight over the road. 'Affordable Water Pumps'."

"Got it. I'll drop by next week."

"Thanks buddy."

He walks back across the road and my pulse rate slowly starts to come down. This can't be doing my blood pressure any good! I grab the step ladder and drive away, breathing a big sigh of relief. Everything is now in place for tonight's big show.

After returning the van, I drive back to the office. There are new cases I should be starting to work on, but I can't focus on anything else at the moment. Everything is going to come down to what happens tonight. If things don't go as planned, my problems with the Eskimos will be even worse than they are now and I will have no choice but to sell up and move away. Of course, if things go badly wrong, I could end up in jail or even dead. I am taking a huge risk, and I'm deeply conflicted. I'm doing things that I never imagined I would do, and I suspect I will have things on my conscience after tonight that I will grapple with for the rest of my life. But I am fully committed now. There will be no turning back. I am a man on a mission, and the primary focus of that mission is the safety of my daughter.

35

———

My alarm wakes me at 4:30 pm. I've slept all afternoon; five solid hours of sleep and I'm feeling much better. I lie in bed for a few more minutes, listening to the sounds of the city as it winds up toward Friday rush hour. A narrow beam of sunlight is slanting diagonally into the darkened room between two slats of the venetian blinds that are slightly apart, and I watch dust motes dancing in lazy circles. I try to imagine Claire lying here with me now, snuggling together on a lazy afternoon, with nothing more to worry about than what takeout to order for dinner and what movie to watch tonight. So much is riding on what will happen in the next few hours.

I told Quinn to try and get some sleep too, because I will need her help tonight. She surfaces soon after I do and by 5:00 pm Karl has arrived as well. The three of us are eating takeout pizza in my lounge room and, as we eat, we go over the details of tonight's operation one last time. A lot will hinge on the timing, and a great deal is beyond our control completely. I am counting on the Reverends to strike back decisively and swiftly. My research revealed a growing tension between the Reverends and the Eskimos in recent months. A series of skirmishes between the two gangs has been reported in the press, as the Reverends continue to expand their territory, and the outnumbered Eskimos appear to be fighting a losing battle. There have been police predictions of a looming major conflict between the two gangs, and I am confident that our raid on their base last night will bring that to a head. My goal last night was to inflict significant damage to their vehicles, while leaving them fully functional. I want the Reverends to be angry and mobile, ready to strike back, hopefully tonight.

"What if they don't come tonight?" asks Karl.

"Then we go again tomorrow night, and every subsequent night until they do. But the Reverends aren't known for their patience. I have a feeling that they'll hit back immediately."

Karl and I leave at 6:00 pm in separate cars, and Quinn stays in my lounge room with her laptop. By 6:40 we are all in place and we settle down to wait. It could be a very long night. Karl is parked in exactly the same spot where we parked last night and is peering into the church parking lot through the gaps in the wooden fence. I am parked a hundred yards from the Eskimos' home base, watching developments there. There will be no dozing tonight. I will need to know the moment the Reverends leave their base, because, if it is late at night, as I suspect it will be, it will only take them twenty minutes to get here, and I will need all of that time to carry out my role.

We check in with each other via a three-way phone link up, every hour on the hour. From the very beginning it is obvious that there is a lot more activity at both gang headquarters. At Eskimo headquarters, hip hop music is blasting from inside and there are a lot more cars tonight, with vehicles parked in the street as well as in their lot. Antonio Sanchez's car is among them. Perhaps it's the big Friday night booze-up. The female entertainment arrives a little after 7:00 and stays for two hours before heading out to solicit business elsewhere.

Meanwhile, over at the church, Karl tells me that there is a very different mood tonight. There is no music coming from the church, and as vehicles arrive and their occupants enter the building Karl spots several shotguns and other firearms in their possession. It definitely looks like tonight is the night.

Quinn has nothing to do until the action starts, but we keep her in the loop.

We've just finished our hourly link-up at midnight and are about to disconnect when Karl interrupts.

"Hold on guys, something's happening!"

There are a few moments of silence and then Karl starts whispering.

"They're all coming out of the church. There must be … hang on … there are at least twenty of them. It's hard to see in the dark. There are lots of weapons in view – people checking their guns and loading ammo. They're getting into their vehicles now and starting their engines. This is it guys! They're leaving now. There are four cars and four bikes. They're coming your way, John! Get going!"

"Can you identify the lead cars?" asks Quinn.

"The lead two vehicles are a dark Chevy Suburban and a dark Ford Ranger. There are a couple of bikes right behind them."

"I'm on it!" she says.

I'm already out of the car and walking briskly up the sidewalk on the opposite side of the street to the Eskimo's shed.

"Quinn, I'll keep the phone to my ear. Give me a progressive report as they move through the CCTV checkpoints."

"Roger."

I'm level with the shed now, and the coast is clear, so I quickly cross the road and slip down the path at the side of the building. Grabbing the can of yellow spray paint from my jacket pocket, I paint a huge Reverend gang tag on the side of the shed. It's an "R" with an extra-long vertical line which is intersected by a short horizontal line near its bottom, forming an inverted cross. I move quickly to the back of the building and paint another one, just to be sure. Then I return to the oxygen bottles to turn them both on, only to find that I can't! The valves are closed so tightly that I can't turn them with my bare hands.

Damn! I should have checked this! I run across the road and back to my car, hoping that I've got a shifter or wrench in my basic car tool kit that I transferred from my old bomb. I wouldn't have a clue what's in it, as I don't think I've ever opened it. I rummage in the boot, while placing Quinn on speaker, hearing her count down the CCTV checkpoints.

Shit! Shit! Shit! Where is the tool kit? Then I find it and, mercifully, there is an adjustable wrench. Abandoning all pretense at subtlety, I race back along the street, only realizing half-way there that I've left my mobile phone in the back of the car. I keep going and make it to the bottles without incident. The wrench works brilliantly and both valves are fully open within seconds. Pure oxygen is now pouring into the front room of the shed, via the wall vent. Yesterday, I had removed the regulator from the gas hose, so the oxygen is now flowing at a rapid rate. I just hope there is enough time for both bottles to completely empty by the time the opposition gang gets here.

I jog up the side of the building and I almost run straight into two gang members who are standing directly out the front of the shed, talking and smoking. I skid to a stop just in time, at the corner of the building and peek around. They haven't heard me because of the loud music, but there's no way I can get passed them while they're standing there. I haven't got my phone, so I don't know how close the Reverends are. *How long did it take me to get to the car, search for the wrench and then get back here?* I just don't know. I wait in the dark at the corner of the building, while the two gang members talk and smoke just outside the front door. *I need to get back to my car and get out of here before the action starts! What the hell are they doing out here?*

What's wrong with their nice warm clubhouse? Maybe they wanted to talk about something in private. I don't know. I can't make out what they're saying because of the hip-hop blaring out the now-open front sliding door.

Minutes go by and at last one of them throws his cigarette butt to the ground and grinds it with his shoe. But instead of going inside, he immediately lights up another one. Damn! These guys are settling in for a long chat, and I can't afford to stay here much longer. If I'm still stuck down the side of this shed when the Reverend's arrive, I'm a dead man.

The two guys are showing no signs of moving and I decide I can't wait any longer. Karl and Quinn are probably freaking out by now because they haven't heard from me for at least ten minutes, but I can't do anything about that. The Reverends must be only a few minutes away and I need to get out of here immediately. I run down the path to the rear of the shed. The path bends around the back and there is a six-foot concrete wall running along the back perimeter, separating the Eskimo's shed from the premises behind. I scale the wall and jump down the other side. I'm now at the rear of a row of factory units that are accessed from the parallel street behind. I run along beside the wall, back in the direction of my car in the other street. After about seventy yards, I come to a side concrete wall separating these factory units from the next lot. I think I need to go another 30 yards to be level with where I parked my car, so I climb the wall and jump down.

I should have checked more carefully before I jumped. It's a small, enclosed yard with another concrete side wall thirty yards further on and a high, chain-link back fence, shared with whatever building is in the street where I parked my car. There are also two vicious guard dogs. I know they're vicious because they immediately launch themselves at me. Adrenaline is a wonderful chemical. It immediately energizes your body, dilating blood vessels, increasing heart rate and blood pressure, dilating the pupils and instantly releasing a huge surge of phos-phocreatine and adenosine triphosphate to your muscles. My feet barely touch the ground before I've leapt like a monkey halfway up the chain-link fence at the rear. Even so, I'm not quite quick enough. One of the dogs, I think it's a German Shepherd, has managed to sink it's teeth into my ass and has torn a piece out of my trousers in the process. I climb the fence, which must be nearly ten feet tall, and misjudge the distance to the ground on the other side, jarring my left ankle as I land.

I haven't got time to think about injuries, however, because I've run out of time. From somewhere further down the road, perhaps the side access street, I can hear a convoy of cars and motorcycles approaching. I'm at the rear of another group of factory units, and I race down the driveway toward the street. I'm directly opposite my car now and I sprint across the road and dive into the car, closing my door just as the first car of the convoy turns into the street from the T-intersection about eighty yards away. I can hear Quinn and Karl yelling frantically through my phone, which is in the back tray of my car, asking if I'm OK. I yell back that I'm alright, but I doubt that they can hear me, because the convoy of SUVs, trucks and motorcycles is roaring past me now, making a hell of a noise.

I hunker down in my seat as the convoy drives past. It's too late for me to start my engine and drive away because I could be mistaken for an Eskimo gang member trying to make an escape. *Damn it! I should have parked further away!* I'll just have to sit it out now and wait for an opportunity to get away.

I don't have to wait long until the action starts. The four cars and four bikes pull up opposite the shed and I can see the two Eskimos still smoking out front, staring at the newcomers. One of them has his cigarette frozen half-way to his lips, all gross motor muscle function momentarily paused as his mind spins its wheels, trying to work out what's happening. The car doors on the far side of the vehicles all open and the occupants pile out, levelling their weapons across the roofs of the cars, while those on the side closest to the shed simply stick their guns out the windows. Then, like a well drilled army, they open fire. It's deafening and the night explodes with a barrage of sound and light.

The two smoking Eskimos don't stand a chance. They are peppered within seconds and are dead before they hit the ground. By the sound of it the Reverends are using some pretty heavy-gauge ammo, and the shed is being literally torn to pieces by their bullets. After a minute or so of continuous barrage, there is a ceasefire, presumably at someone's command, and immediately two Reverends run across the road with flaming bottles in their hands and launch them through the now shattered windows. The ceasefire has obviously enabled some surviving Eskimos to raise their heads above ground level, and several shots are fired from inside as the two home-made bombs arc toward them. One of the Reverends cops one in the center of his chest and falls to the ground, fatally wounded, just as the explosion occurs.

And what an explosion it is.

Normally a Molotov cocktail will explode in a spectacular but limited fashion, its flaming fuel burning those within a ten-yard radius. But this explosion is of another order entirely. Pure oxygen is a volatile gas which, although not explosive by itself, will dramatically increase the effects of an explosion. The Eskimo gang would not have noticed the build-up of oxygen in their shed, as it is a completely odorless gas, but they were effectively sitting in a ticking time bomb.

My research had discovered that Molotov cocktails were the calling card of the Reverends. The gang referred to them as 'baptism by fire', in keeping with their religious mimicry, and the fiery bombs were a favourite weapon in their clashes with rival gangs.

The explosion practically lifts the shed into orbit. Windows in surrounding buildings are shattered, and my car is rocked on its suspension although I am a hundred yards away. No one inside could have survived that blast. The Reverends have all been injured as well, either by the compression wave from the blast or from flying debris. Those who were out of their vehicles or standing beside their motorcycles are now lying all over the sidewalk, and the car windows have all been blown in.

Maybe I only needed one bottle of oxygen.

I quickly climb over the back of the car, retrieve my phone, then start my engine and drive away, leaving my lights off until I have turned into the side street and I'm out of sight. There is no chance of being chased by the Reverends. Most of them are barely conscious.

But the cops are another matter.

"John! Where are you?!" asks Quinn.

"I'm just leaving now. The whole place went up like a rocket!"

The plan was for me to leave as soon as I turned on the gas bottles, in order to get as far away as possible before the action started. Me being here now is not part of the plan.

"John! The cops are coming! I'm tracking them on CCTV. Give me your exact location."

I tell her, and she is silent for a few seconds.

"Make a U-turn immediately!"

I don't hesitate, ripping the wheel around and applying the handbrake. The back wheels slide around spectacularly, and I gun the engine to straighten it up. Where are the Hollywood cameras when you need them?

"First left!" Quinn yells.

I turn left and then I hear her swear.

"That might not be any good either! I've lost them between two cameras! Turn into a driveway and switch your engine off! Do it now!"

I do as she says. I'm only just in time. A series of police cars turn into the street and come racing past, red and blue lights flashing and sirens screaming.

A few moments later they've passed, and I tell Quinn.

"OK," she says. "Now get the hell out of there!"

So I get the hell out of there.

36

I t's 1:45 am, and we are back in my lounge room, completely wired with post-op adrenaline. I have it the worst. My hands are shaking and I'm feeling slightly dazed. Only after arriving back home do I notice that I am injured more seriously than I realized. I have a nasty bite wound in my right buttock that is quite deep, with a flap of flesh that needs suturing. Fortunately, I called in at a pharmacy yesterday and bought some more surgical sutures, so I have everything necessary to patch myself up. The only problem is, I can't reach the wound.

"One of you is going to have to do it for me," I say to Karl and Quinn.

They both look at me as if I've asked them to rip their own heads off.

"No way, dude! I'm not going anywhere near your ass!" says Karl.

"Me either!" agrees Quinn. "A hundred bucks a week isn't nearly enough to get me to touch your ass."

"It's not like I've got leprosy or something!" I complain. "Come on Karl! We both did emergency first aid in our basic training. You can handle it."

"I refuse to handle any guy's ass, bro!"

"So you'd be OK touching a girl's butt, would you?" I ask.

Karl leans over and examines Quinn's ass in an exaggerated fashion.

"Yeah. For instance, I'd be very happy to sew up Quinn's ass if she needed it."

"Thanks, man," she says, holding her beer bottle out toward him.

"My pleasure," he replies clinking bottles with her.

"Come on, guys! I'm slowly dying here! Help me out."

In the end – quite literally – they start working together on the wound. Karl injects the local anesthetic, Quinn cleans the wound with antiseptic, Karl stitches it up, and they both work together in applying a bandage over it. Of course, they keep up a running commentary as they work.

"He's quite hairy, isn't he?" comments Quinn as I lay face down on the lounge.

"I'd describe it as a covering of soft down, rather than actual hair," replies Karl.

"They're nicely toned buttocks, though, aren't they?" adds Quinn.

"Yeah," replies Karl, "I've always said he has a nice butt."

Karl eventually goes home and Quinn heads downstairs to her own bed. By 2:30 I'm lying in bed trying to sleep, but my mind remains active. I can't stop thinking about what I've done. Many people have died tonight. I didn't pull the trigger, but I may as well have. I guess it could be argued that there was bound to be violence between the two gangs. It definitely was a matter of 'when' rather than 'if'. I can also take some comfort in the fact that many of the Eskimos, perhaps most, would have already been dead by the time of the explosion, killed by the deadly hail of bullets from the Reverends' guns. Their deaths are the result of a violent war between two rival criminal gangs. But I have to face the reality that some of them may have survived the battle if I had not filled their shed with a highly combustible gas. I am directly complicit in at least some of the deaths.

I will have to live with this.

However, despite the sobering weight of this knowledge, I can't help feeling a great sense of relief and elation. My daughter and I are now free from the threat of harm from these violent criminals. We are free to live our lives without constantly looking over our shoulders. I don't have to live in the paralyzing fear of coming home one day to find that Addie is missing or that something terrible has happened to her. It is this overwhelming sense of relief that finally floods my soul and allows me to drift off into sleep.

37

The news services the next morning are practically salivating over the story of the overnight gang violence. It makes national and even international headlines. As the morning progresses, the full details of last night's battle are gradually revealed. There are eighteen dead and twelve injured. Sixteen of the dead are Eskimos, which, according to the best estimates by various news sources, represents their entire gang. Police made fourteen arrests last night and are still actively searching for four more Reverends who escaped and remain on the run. The San Jose police chief makes an appearance at around 9:00 am and talks about senseless gang violence, but also intimates that this is a very good day for the people of San Jose and Santa Clara as, in one single night, two whole gangs have effectively been wiped from the map.

"Our citizens can walk safer in the streets today and sleep safer in their beds tonight, as a result of last night's horrendous gun battle," he says.

Local residents report hearing a massive explosion during the battle, and the clean-up that is now starting in the area indicates that it was a significant blast. Damage to surrounding businesses, however, is minimal, largely limited to broken windows. Forensic investigators are still combing the scene trying to determine the cause of the blast but they suspect that there may have been a gas leak which contributed to it.

Costa can talk of nothing else as he makes my morning coffee.

"It is the hand of God, my friend!" he says. "Lydia and me, we pray every night now for the safety of our shop and for you too, Mr. John, and for Addie. And look what happens, eh? God answers, my friend. God always answers!"

"He certainly does, Costa."

"Ah, this is a good day, Mr. John! A very good day!"

By the time I get back to the office, Quinn has downed her morning sludge and is wearing a tight black dress. I'm stunned. I've only ever seen her in jeans and a T-shirt.

Before I can open my mouth, she points an accusing finger at me and says, "Don't say a word! Not a word!"

I hold my hands up in mock surrender.

"I wouldn't dare! Where are you off to?" I ask, unable to keep the surprise out of my voice.

"Wedding. I'm the photographer."

"Ah. I see. You're joining the ranks of the bourgeois in search of the filthy lucre. Everyone compromises in the end, eh?"

"I can think of worse ways of making a buck," she replies. "I get free food and drink and I help people celebrate the happiest day of their lives. I'll settle for that."

"Well said," I reply. "And thanks for last night. I couldn't have done it without your help."

"My pleasure. How's your butt?"

"Good. How's yours?"

"I think it looks pretty damn good in this dress, don't you?" she says, turning around and giving me a decent view of it.

"As your employer, I refuse to answer that question on the

grounds that my response could be construed as sexual harassment."

"I'll take that as a yes," she says, smiling. And then she does something that completely surprises me. She walks over and gives me a kiss on the cheek. "You're a good man, John Targett. Don't beat yourself up about what you had to do last night. The world is a better place this morning because of you. And your daughter is safe, now. Be at peace, dude."

She leaves shortly after, hitching a pair of baggy trousers on over her dress and donning a leather jacket before firing up her V-Star Cruiser and roaring off down the back lane. I stand in the office for a while in the silence, looking around me and savoring this moment. We are safe. Costa and his business are safe. Addie will be back home with me tonight, and we can resume our life together. What is more, the long rift between me and Addie's grandparents seems to be healing. It feels like a new beginning. A fresh start. And Claire looms large in that picture for me. Something wonderful has begun, and I don't want it to stop.

I am in the midst of my reflections when there is a light tap at the door and I look up to see Detective Elijah Abrams standing in the doorway.

"You look like a man deep in thought."

"Looks can be deceptive, Detective."

"Indeed they can, indeed they can," he says, giving me a piercing look. Why do I always get the impression that he can read my mind?

"Can I help you?" I ask, but he doesn't immediately answer. Instead, he shuffles over to my desk and sits in the padded visitor's chair, pointing me toward my own chair as he does so. I get the hint and walk to the desk, taking my seat and facing him across the desk. He has a clean shirt on today. Maybe he washes his shirts once a month and today is the first day of the new shirt. It's a pity he doesn't wash his cardigan though, as I think I can see a fresh beetroot stain on his left cuff.

"Something you want to talk about?" I try again.

"You must be very pleased with this morning's news," he begins.

"Shocked and pleased in equal measure."

"I'm sure you are."

He looks around at my office and stares at the striped curtain covering the access to the rear rooms.

"You really should get rid of that God-awful curtain, you know."

"I suppose I should, but then again, it does give people something to talk about when there's a lull in the conversation."

He merely nods.

"You know, this morning is one of the best mornings I've had in a long time," he says. "Possibly one of the best days in my whole policing career. I can't remember a day in the past when so many bad guys did us all a favor and permanently removed themselves from the gene pool. By the time we catch these four other morons who are still on the run – and we will – a total of thirty-six gang members will have been removed from our streets in a single night."

"That's a very good result," I say.

"It's goddam brilliant!"

He pauses for a moment and gives a long, satisfied sigh.

"I just wanted to drop over and tell you that you won't be troubled by that gang anymore. They're all dead. The only one left alive is going to be rotting in jail for a very long time."

"That's a great relief," I say.

"What are you doing tomorrow for lunch?"

The question completely throws me off balance.

"Lunch?" I ask.

"Yes. It's a strange tradition where people eat food in the middle of the day to replenish their calories."

"Yes, I'm vaguely familiar with the practice. I'm not doing anything in particular."

"Good. Would you like to have lunch with me at the Sergeants Arms? It's my favorite pub. I usually have lunch there on a Sunday."

"Um, yeah, sure. Thanks. I'd like that."

"Alright. Let's say twelve noon."

"OK."

He gets up and walks to the door, then turns and looks at me curiously.

"Here's a funny thing for you. There's a factory unit in the street behind where last night's mayhem took place. They manufacture jewelry for several local jewelry stores. They've had a few robberies recently, and so they keep guard dogs locked up there at night. They also have security cameras all around their unit. On a whim we asked to see their footage from last night."

"Oh yes?" I say, my mouth suddenly going dry.

"Yes. It turns out that just before things went crazy, someone in dark clothing climbed the side wall, jumped into the rear of the premises and had a near scrape with the dogs."

"Did he?"

"He barely escaped. Looks like he got bitten on the behind."

"Sounds painful."

"Mm. Managed to climb the back fence and ran down the driveway toward the street where the action happened."

"Very peculiar."

"Yes. Isn't it? I couldn't help noticing, however, that he had a watchband just like yours. Couldn't make out the watch, of course. Too dark. Too dark to see his face too. But that blue watchband of yours with the reflective white stripe down the middle is quite distinctive, isn't it? I've never seen anyone else wearing one."

"Really? I see them all the time. They're a dime a dozen. Every second jogger is wearing them these days."

"Is that so? Well, I guess I'm just out of touch with current trends." He scratches his head. I hope he doesn't have head lice, because I'm having lunch with him tomorrow.

"Our forensic team found two gas bottles at the side of the shed, with a hose that looked like it had been stuck into a vent. The bottles been painted over, but the serial numbers have been traced. They were oxygen bottles, purchased from a local supplier by the Reverends - at least that's what the paperwork says."

He gives me a curious look.

"You know, pure oxygen is a very volatile gas," he says.

"Is that so? I didn't know that."

"Didn't you?" He pauses. "The thing is, none of the gang members we arrested seem to know anything about the gas bottles."

"That's what drugs will do to your brain," I suggest. "They ruin your short term memory. It's a wonder those guys can work out which shoe goes on which foot when they get dressed."

Abrams merely nods.

"You know, if it turns out that someone set that whole thing up last night – set one gang against another – I reckon that person would deserve a medal." He fixes me with that piercing gaze of his again.

"I suppose he would," I agree, "but I find it hard to believe that anyone could have done that."

"I suppose so." He nods thoughtfully. "Yes, I suppose it is a bit of a stretch." He gives me a smile. He really shouldn't do that; it doesn't suit him in the slightest. It makes him look as though he has a bad case of constipation.

"Well, I'll be going. See you tomorrow."

Abrams walks out the office door into the foyer and turns back to me one last time as he reaches the door to the street.

"Oh, by the way, that butt of yours seems to be very painful. I couldn't help noticing you wincing as you sat down. You might want to get that looked at. You don't want to get an infection. Dog bites can be very nasty."

With that, he steps through the door and shuffles down the sidewalk, leaving me stunned.

He's a cunning old bastard. But I think I've just made a new friend.

38

———————

Two weeks later I'm setting up for my first police training session at the Santa Clara Fitness Center, a new gym which has recently opened just a couple of blocks from the police station. As an act of community service, the owners of the gym have donated the use of their large, rubber-floored cross fit room for a two-hour session once a month. Because this whole thing was Abrams's idea, the police chief has given him the responsibility of organizing and running it. Consequently, he is here with me today, marking off names as the men and women who have been rostered on for this training session gradually arrive. While he does that, I am getting the dummies and body pads out of the storeroom and spreading mats around. The dummies and pads have been purchased by the police department and donated to the gym as a reciprocal act of generosity.

Eventually all twenty attendees are present and are standing in groups, chatting, dressed in appropriate gym clothes. Abrams gets their attention and briefly outlines his expectation to them. He explains that they will be rostered on to attend two of these sessions every year and that their satisfactory participation in the classes will be considered essential for their ongoing employment as police officers. I sense a distinct lack of enthusiasm among the group, even resentment in some individuals. Abrams then briefly introduces me, citing my previous national titles in mixed martial arts. It doesn't seem to overly-impress the group and I notice a couple of eye rolls and smirks. This is going to be a tough group.

I was planning to start with some basic aerobic warm-up exercises before commencing self-defense techniques, but after sensing the group's less than enthusiastic attitude I change my plan. I walk to the center of the room and ask them to gather around me in a wide circle. I've already identified my target. He's the biggest guy in the room, obviously a gym junkie, at least three inches taller than me, thirty pounds heavier and biceps like tree trunks. He's also one of the eye-rollers and smirkers.

"You, sir. What's your name?"

"Gavin," he replies, with a surly tone.

"Gavin, would you mind stepping forward and being part of the first demo?"

His buddies on either side laugh and slap him on the back. He shrugs and steps forward, and ends up standing directly in front of me, still with a smirk on his face. I ask him to put a body pad on, which consists of a vest with front and rear pads. When he's adjusted it properly and I've checked it for fit I step back and face him.

"OK, now I'd like you to hit me."

A brief look of puzzlement crosses his face, and there are some laughs and hoots from a couple of his buddies.

"You want me to hit you?"

"Yes please."

"Where?"

"Let's try a punch to the head, shall we?"

"Seriously?"

"Yes please. Whenever you're ready."

He shakes his head in mild disbelief as his buddies laugh and hoot some more. "OK."

He swings a right hook at my head and I use a classic evasion technique, leaning back, twisting to the right and brushing his arm aside at the same time. I step back and shake my head at him.

"Gavin, Gavin, Gavin," I say, condescendingly. "You can do a whole lot better than that. That wasn't a punch, it was a swat. My grandmother can do better than that. I want you to put some effort into it please. Give me all you've got."

He's stopped smirking now and wears a more serious expression. His eyes narrow and he clenches both fists. I've poked the bear.

He swings again, much harder and faster, but I'm ready for it. Instead of leaning away and swatting his arm down, this time I step inside and pivot to the left, grabbing his arm as his fist flies past my face. I dig my right hip into his abdomen and use his momentum to throw him. He lands with a thud on the mat behind me. His mates are laughing again, but this time it's at his expense, not mine.

Gavin stands and looks more than a little cross. I make sure he isn't injured and ask him if he would like to try one more time. He's now fully motivated and can't decline without losing face in front of his mates. We square up again and this time he assumes a classic boxing stance, with both arms up, his left leading and his right a little behind, cocked and loaded. He's moving on his toes now, and it's obvious he's had some boxing training. He feints once, then once again, and all the while I'm just standing there with my arms by my side, presenting him with an open target.

Finally, he makes his move. He leads with a left jab with the clear intention of following up with a right haymaker. But I don't let him get that far. As the left jab comes at me, I pivot on the ball of my right foot and bend at the waist. As his jab passes harmlessly over the top of my right shoulder, I complete the pivot, swinging my left leg around and kicking him squarely in the chest. Gavin is a big guy and I needed to put a lot of power into the kick to knock him off his feet. I hope I didn't overdo it and break a rib, because Gavin flies backward and lands on his back on the mat behind him. The group is completely silent now. I have their full attention.

I walk over to Gavin and as he stands, I offer him my outstretched hand.

"Thanks, Gavin. You're a good sport."

He considers his options for a moment then grudgingly shakes my hand. As he goes back to the group, I address them.

"The point of that demonstration wasn't to show off or prove how good I am. It was simply to demonstrate that good technique beats strength and power every time. In two sessions a year I can't hope to turn you into martial arts experts, but I'm confident that I can impart some simple skills and techniques that might one day either save your life or stop you from having to use deadly force. All I ask is that you treat these sessions seriously and that you give one hundred percent while you're here."

The group is completely with me now, and I can see Abrams standing off to the side, with one of his weird grins on his face.

I clap my hands. "OK! Let's begin!"

Two hours later, the last of the group has left and Abrams and I are packing the last of the dummies away.

"Thanks Doc," he says. I haven't been able to convince him to call me anything else.

"My pleasure."

"Are you sure you don't want to invoice us for your time."

"No. I'm happy to donate my time. It's a worthwhile cause."

He nods and pats my back. "OK. I'll see you on the weekend."

Fifteen minutes later, I'm back in the office. Quinn has gone out for lunch and I'm thinking of heading upstairs to make a sandwich when there is a knock at the door. It takes me all of two seconds to recognize my visitor as an FBI agent. There must be a factory somewhere that rolls them off an assembly line, looking identical.

"Can I help you?" I ask.

He steps inside the door and approaches my desk.

"John Targett?"

"That's me."

He flashes me his ID.

"I'm Senior Special Agent Frank Morrison, from the San Francisco office of the FBI."

"Please, take a seat. What can I do for you, Agent Morrison? I'm guessing it's about the information I sent you on the baby swapping racquet."

He sits and crosses his legs, striking a casual pose.

"Yes. That's quite an impressive file you managed to put together."

"Thanks. I hope it was helpful."

"Very." He pauses. "Obviously, I'm not at liberty to discuss our ongoing investigation into the matter, but I wanted to meet you to firstly assure you that we are taking the matter very seriously. A team of agents has been assigned to the case and we are making steady progress. There will be a number of indictments that will eventually result from this."

"I'm glad to hear it."

There is another pause in the conversation, so I prompt him.

"You said 'firstly'. Is there a second reason why you've dropped by?"

"I'm curious."

"Curiosity is, in great and generous minds, the first passion and the last."

Morrison raises his eyebrows, enquiringly.

"Samuel Johnson," I explain.

"Ah. I see." He nods thoughtfully. "My curiosity is of a more prosaic nature. I'm wondering how you managed to come by your information."

I sit back and clasp my hands together. I was anticipating this question.

"A little birdie told me."

"Your little birdie must be extremely clever."

"Avian intelligence is highly underrated."

"The thing is," he continues, disregarding my flippant quip, "some of that digital information resides on secure servers. The only way it could have been obtained is via unauthorized access to those servers."

"Really? That's shocking. That's a crime, isn't it?"

"Yes. Unlawfully accessing a computer system and obtaining unauthorized information can attract a prison sentence of one to five years."

"And so it should," I say. "We don't want people nosing around in our private information, willy-nilly."

"Indeed."

He pauses.

"In this case, of course, the information that was unlawfully gathered was extremely helpful to us in uncovering a serious and ongoing international criminal operation. We are inclined not to pursue the identity of the source any further. We've got bigger fish to fry."

"You're choosing to fry the fish rather than net the birdie."

"Precisely."

"That's very civilized of you," I say. "Little birdies deserve to be protected."

He merely nods his head.

"Have you ever considered a career with the Bureau?" he asks.

I raise my eyebrows. I wasn't expecting that.

"No. Can't say that I have."

Morrison reaches into his top pocket and hands me his card.

"If you ever want to discuss the possibility, give me a call."

He stands and reaches across the desk to shake my hand.

"It was good to meet you. And thanks again for the information."

He walks to the door and pauses before leaving.

"By the way, if you happen to ever see that little birdie again, tell it to be a good citizen from now on and stick to its own nest."

"I'll be sure to pass the message on."

"Good."

He nods his head and leaves. The FBI has just gone up a couple of notches in my estimation.

It's been a month since the 'Night of the Bomb' and life hasn't really returned to normal. I don't think it ever will, because that's the nature of life, isn't it? It shifts and changes, and just when you think you've got it all worked out, it shifts again. I'm living in a new normal now, and I like it – mostly.

Quinn's got me drinking green slime in the mornings. That's a part of the new normal that I'm still not sure about. I'll give it another week. Quinn has also somehow got Addie eating brussels sprouts and carrots. This is a minor miracle. I'm not sure how she did it, and I don't even dare comment about it in case I break the spell.

Addie has a boyfriend now. He wears socks and flip flops on his feet and I can always see what brand of underwear he's got on. His name is Joel, he has acne, is sixteen and is apparently 'lit'. They've been out twice to the movies. My first words to him when I met him were, "Hello Joel. I'm Addie's father. I have a gun. Always remember that."

Elijah Abrams and I have struck up a surprising friendship. He's a gruff old bugger, but we have an easy camaraderie and nothing more has ever been said about the 'Night of the Bomb'.

We meet every Sunday for a pub lunch and a game of pool at the Sergeants Arms. He is a triple divorcee who has given up on the idea of marriage but he apparently has a 'friend with benefits' whom he sees every Saturday night. I don't want to know any more details. He and Addie have hit it off too. He occasionally drops in for a cup of coffee and a chat in the afternoons, and Addie has been showing him how to use Facebook.

Tonight, Claire is hosting a dinner party for me; just a small circle of friends. It's my 40th birthday. This is not something I particularly want to celebrate, but the nature of birthdays is that the birthday-ee has the least say in how or even *if* it is celebrated. He must simply grin and bear it while everyone else inflicts their joyful celebration upon him.

Addie and I arrive a little after 6:00, because she had a 3:30 soccer match that started late, and part of her growing older is that she must now apparently stay in the shower until every drop of hot water has been completely used up. I'm not sure why.

Everyone else is already there when we arrive: Karl and Billie, Elijah Abrams and Quinn. They all make an initial fuss about me when I walk in, with numerous references to 'birthday boy' and 'old man' intermingled. They forget about me a few moments later, however, and resume their previous conversations, allowing me to slip into the kitchen and receive a much more enjoyable birthday welcome from Claire. She is looking absolutely stunning tonight and I still can't believe how lucky I am to have found someone as intelligent and witty and gorgeous as she.

I am asked to sit in the lounge room while everyone gives me presents, like a King being honored by his subjects. I specifically commanded these particular subjects to do no such thing, but they have flagrantly disobeyed me. What's the point of being King if no one listens to you?

Quinn gives me a book entitled, 'Angry Birds for Dummies'.

Abrams has bought me a pool cue, for our regular Sunday games. Billie and Karl give me a voucher for two night's accommodation at a luxury hotel, including all meals, redeemable anytime in the next twelve months.

"The only trouble is," says Billie, winking at me, "you'll have to think of someone to take with you, because it's a reservation for two."

"Do you want to come with me, Karl?" I ask, and receive a thump on the arm from Claire, who is sitting beside me.

Addie has bought me a book entitled, 'How to Understand Women: A Simple Guide for Neanderthals', which will no doubt be very helpful.

Finally, I unwrap Claire's present. It's not so much a present as a legal contract.

"You have to sign it," she says.

I read it aloud to the whole group.

"I, John Targett, hereby give Claire Peters complete authority to redecorate my office. I promise not to whine or complain or question her judgment, as I fully acknowledge my complete ineptitude regarding interior design."

Everyone laughs and applauds, and I sign my name with a regal flourish, receiving a kiss from Claire in return.

Dinner is served soon after, and we sit around Claire's large dining table eating a selection of my favorite food, mostly involving various forms of dead animal – aquatic and terrestrial.

Abrams (apparently everyone calls him by his surname) has washed his cardigan for the occasion which, more than anything else, tells me what a special event my birthday is.

I am able to sit down without wincing now. Claire, of course, sussed out my injury almost immediately on that first Saturday and insisted on inspecting the wound. It was not exactly how I envisaged the circumstances surrounding her first glimpse of my bottom, but what can you do? She later assured me that I had passed the 'bottom test' in her list of criteria for the ideal man. I've no idea what else is on the list.

I had to tell Claire what happened on the 'Night of the Bomb', as I couldn't potentially start a life with her while holding onto such a terrible secret. It was a difficult conversation and she spent a couple of days mulling it over as she considered whether I was the sort of man she wanted to continue spending time with. She finally decided that if she was ever in danger, she would want a man who would move heaven and earth to keep her safe.

As we sit around the table eating, Quinn and Addie are engaged in a deep discussion about a rapper who is 'totally dank', Abrams is debating handguns with Karl, claiming that nothing beats the Smith and Wesson because it never jams, and Billie and Claire are talking about a book that they have to finish reading for this week's book club. I take a moment to think how lucky I am to have this family of friends.

Eventually Claire brings out a birthday cake and I manage to blow out all the candles. This apparently means that I am now allowed to live for another year. I am asked to give a speech, and I already know what I'm going to say. After thanking them for their good wishes and their gifts, I drop the bombshell and announce that, yesterday, Claire foolishly agreed to marry me. This elicits much joy and congratulations, as well as commiserations from Karl who tells Claire that she still has time to back out. Claire, of course is crying because I give a little speech about how much I love her, and I also thank Billie and Karl for bringing us together.

It is late in the evening when I finally manage to corner Quinn and have a conversation with her alone.

"OK. Out with it. Spill the beans."

"What beans?"

"Whatever it is that's bugging you. You haven't been yourself all night."

"It's nothing. It can wait until tomorrow."

"No, it can't. I want to know now. It's my birthday and you're not allowed to be sad."

"It's precisely because it is your birthday that I don't want to tell you!"

"Now you've got to tell me. I won't take no for an answer."

"OK, but I'm warning you, you won't like it."

"I don't care; out with it!"

"Well, since it's your birthday today, I was fiddling around on the computer and I remember you told me that you were born in O'Connor Hospital. So, I kind of hacked into their birth records and I found yours."

"Kind of hacked or actually hacked?"

"Actually."

"OK. So?"

"So, everything in your record has been deleted."

"Deleted?"

"Yeah. Just like Cory's was."

I shake my head, trying to process what she's saying.

"So, then I hacked into the CLNS, the California Laboratory for Neonatal Screening, and checked the dates around your birthday."

"And?"

"And you're not going to like it."

"Tell me."

"Two days after your supposed birthday, you tested positive for severe SMA – spinal muscular atrophy. It's an incurable malformation of the spinal cord which causes escalating muscle weakness and paralysis. They also recorded a notation from the hospital that you were born with congenital heart disease."

"But I don't have those things."

"No. You don't."

Quinn is staring at me now, watching my reaction, a look of deep concern on her face.

And that's when it happens. My world shifts again. A realignment of monumental proportions. The universe spins on its axis and everything I thought I understood about who I am vanishes.

Because, just like Cory Wainwright, I've been living someone else's life.

THE END

LEAVE A REVIEW

If you enjoyed this book, I would be extremely grateful if you would leave a review on Amazon, Goodreads and other review websites. Reviews are hugely important for me as a self-published author. Every single review really does help!

Leaving a review is very easy. To leave a review, just click the links below. A review of 4 or 5 stars is considered to be a positive review and a review of 3 or less stars is considered to be a negative review. (Amazon will only allow you to leave a review if you have made some verified purchases on their website during the preceding 12 months, but anyone can write a review on Goodreads).

<u>LEAVE A REVIEW:</u>

AMAZON

GOODREADS

ALSO BY KEVIN SIMINGTON

Book I in the STARPATH series

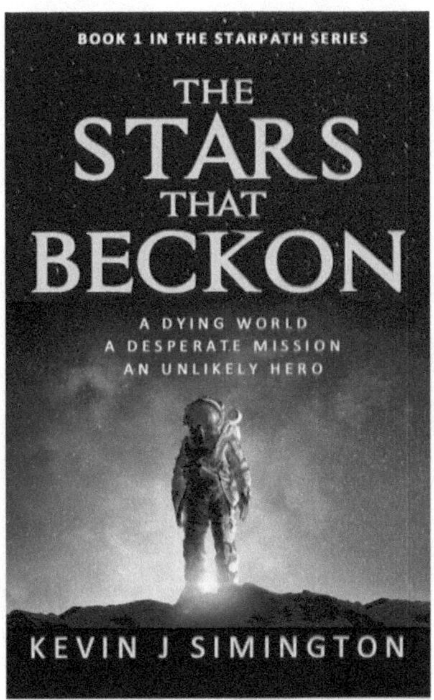

GET IT HERE

Read the highly acclaimed series that has everyone talking! A ragged band of desperate survivors flee from a dying world in search of a new home.

"Incredibly well written, intelligent science fiction that will grip you and not let go. You won't be able to put it down!" - Amazon Reviewer.

THE SPECTACULAR NEW "LONGSHOT SERIES"

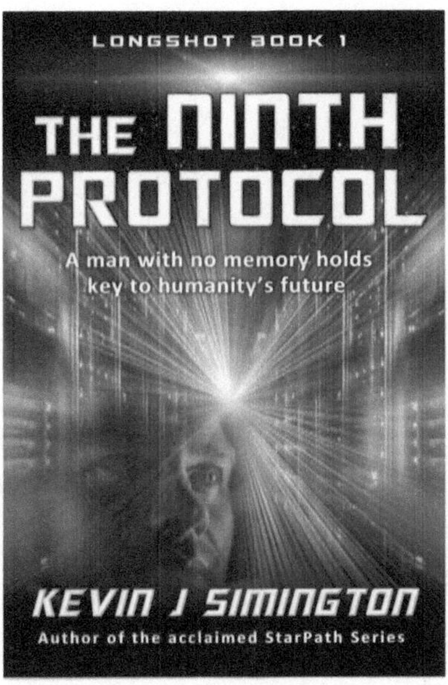

GET IT HERE

A spine-tingling, high-tech thriller by a highly acclaimed, emerging voice in science fiction. Set in the spacefaring 24th century, this is an electrifying story that asks chillingly important questions about the morality and limits of possible human modification.

ALL 3 BOOKS IN THE SERIES ARE OUT NOW!

FREE EBOOK!

Join my mailing list and receive a FREE EBOOK. I will email you a complimentary copy of "**Welcome To The Universe: A Pocket Guide For Visitors**". With stunning photographs and mind-boggling facts, the book provides a fascinating glimpse into the wonders of the universe and the many challenges of space travel. Just click the link below and tell me where to send your free copy (or sign up to my mailing list at kevinsimington.com).

SEND ME A FREE COPY OF "WELCOME TO THE UNIVERSE"

ABOUT THE AUTHOR

Kevin J Simington is an acclaimed fiction and non-fiction author whose books are renowned for their intelligence, clarity and wit. He is a very popular conference speaker on the topics of philosophy, apologetics and science. He also writes for several international magazines.

Website:
https://kevinsimington.com

Amazon Author Page:
amazon.com/author/kevinjsimington

www.ingramcontent.com/pod-product-compliance
Lightning Source LLC
Chambersburg PA
CBHW050152120726
47903CB00002B/598